DOMINION

An Apocalyptic Epic in Seven Books

BOOK I

SEED

by

Compasse

Sacrata Dei Press
A Division of The Compasse Corporation

Front Cover Art: *Gathering Storm*, by Ben Hamrick

Back Cover Art: *Satan Falls*, by Gustave Doré

Printed in the United States of America

For John Karol Mary, Jacinta Christopher, Gianna Anthony, & David Guadalupe;

I pray that I may one day see the marvelous vision that you now embrace...

Author's Note

This manuscript is completely a work of fiction. Though I have enjoyed engaging in an ongoing reflection on the "signs of the times" during my brief tenure on this earth, ultimately, when it comes to "the end", I defer to the words of Christ, who claimed, "no one knows the day or hour... except my Father in Heaven." The very nature of prophecy is that it cannot be predicted nor fully understood by human reason alone until its fulfillment. On this basis, I am confident that the scenario presented here will *not* be the manner in which events leading toward the close of the age will unfold. Truly, for those who count themselves among the Believers, the foretold Second Coming is and will continue to be a *mystery*, unraveling gradually, yet deliberately, in our midst.

So why write this story at all? Well, first and foremost, this very tale has been cathartic for me—even a source of conversion. It is difficult to delve into the mysteries of the Christian Faith without being transformed. Its genesis began with a thought that struck me many years ago as I stood at the threshold of adolescence; what exactly is the *character* of music? How is it that a series of sustained sounds, formed and combined into certain patterns, has the power to tickle the senses and stir the emotions—yet transcending each, reaching out to touch the *Divine*? And what then of the man who discovers the intricate secrets of its language so as to harness its power? Could he not then move mountains?

The question enraptured me, and over the years that followed—some very dark, some that included fleeting moments of happiness—my thoughts would return to the role of music in the human drama. Could this medium reveal a deeper purpose in life...even a bridge to a world unseen? And if so, could it not then provide a common thread that might speak of events to come?

Though the answers continued to elude me, a storyline began to form—even wrestle—within me (often times without my permission). As the years passed and the story fermented, a second purpose for extracting the tale and "giving the words flesh" began to emerge. I found that fewer and fewer people seemed to be asking the great questions of existence: Why am I here? What lies beyond the veil of death? What is truth? On the one hand, I found some who attempted to provide neat, pat, "Christian-Pop" answers that felt superficial and seemed only to validate the individual's lifestyle and worldview. But even more so, on the opposing hand, I witnessed what

Father Charles Arminjon described (as far back as the nineteenth century) as a "terrifying indifference and profound universal lethargy" when it came to questions pertaining to our place in existence, the maneuverings of men of power in our civilization, and the reflection on those things that exist beyond the senses. It appeared that the words of the prophet Daniel regarding the two old men of Babylon could be applied to us all: "They suppressed their consciences; they would not allow their eyes to look to heaven, and did not keep in mind God's just judgments."

So I pressed forward, extracting thoughts and scenarios, finding in the process that they preferred to take on a life on their own. To be clear, I neither was nor am a theologian, philosopher, or biblical scholar—and I am definitely not a prophet! At best, I continue to be a fellow traveler on the journey of life, seeking meaning in this existence, trying to wade through all the illusions and deceptions in order to get to the central, unifying Truth. On this road, I have found myself most drawn towards those who do not necessarily provide all the answers I seek outright, but who possess the humility to acknowledge that the sometimes-elusive truths of existence cannot be fully answered by reason alone; on this side of eternity, *mystery* reigns supreme. I pray that this work reflects this sentiment.

One final note that I feel I would be remiss in not offering; evil, in its deepest forms of self-corrupted good, is uncomfortable, twisted, and vile. In my experiences in life, I have been witness to many strains of this depravity and have come to believe that any attempts at sanitizing the reality of iniquity in order to make it more palatable to the reader is to do a disservice to the Truth. Therefore, the presentation of disturbing manifestations of evil—within images, acts, and language—has remained intact. Truly, this work is unsettling—especially to the Believer—and in reality, the Believer is *not* the intended audience.

If the words on this page appear too endowed with religious language for your own taste, then perhaps this manuscript is for you. If the words do not go far enough, it is very likely that reading this tale would only serve to rob you of your peace. I humbly offer this work for both your discretion and your discernment.

– Compasse

What if . . . .

Prologue

...the Earth shook.

Ibn was sure of it. Just a moment before, he had been standing on the rotting stump of an olive tree, playing an Arab version of 'King of the Mountain' with his friends. He had paused momentarily—thinking he had heard the faint sound of...*music*. Now he was lying on his back, shaking off a sudden spell of vertigo. As he looked around the place where he lay, he saw his friends staring at each other with various strained expressions of disbelief.

Ibn picked himself up off the ground and had begun the process of brushing the dust from his clothes when something peculiar caught his eye. There, high atop the Western Wall (or the Wailing Wall, as his Jewish friends would often correct him), stood two figures. On occasion, he remembered seeing soldiers moving along the same spot, sporting their automatic rifles, "keeping the peace" as some would say. And each day thousands of Jews and tourists would flock below, slipping their written prayers into the crevices of the wall, while thousands of Muslims would ascend Mount Moriah, entering through the Western Gate to worship at *Al Aksa*, the most ancient Mosque of the Islamic faith. The multitude was even greater today, as a great mass of pilgrims were celebrating the peculiar Christian Holy Day of Epiphany.

But there was something curious—even mysterious—about these two men who stood upon the same Mount this day. The first was meticulously dressed in what even Ibn could recognize as stately clothing, worn only by the very wealthy or the very powerful. The second, in stark contrast, looked as if he had just crawled out of a sewer, wearing some tattered material that may at one time have been indicative of the very poor. Yet as they stood together gazing at the winter sky, it would seem as if their acquaintance was the most natural event to have ever occurred in the history of mankind.

Suddenly, there again, Ibn heard the distinct sound of music. He darted his head in all directions, desperately attempting to ascertain the origin of this peculiar song. Then, as if to quell any of Ibn's prior doubts, the Earth trembled once again. This time, however, there was no question about it. He fell to the ground, terrified as the thundering sound of a thousand chariots rumbled throughout the land. Ear-piercing wails of the multitude rang out, and Ibn watched helplessly as large crevices broke open on the Mount.

Then, just as quickly as it had all started, the Earth became still. Ibn again picked himself up—determined this would be the last time this day that he would be on the ground—and began once again to brush himself off. The momentary silence was then broken as he heard a chorus of cries from atop Mount Moriah.

Having quickly forgotten the pair of surreal figures he had seen atop the Mount, Ibn looked up. His youthful curiosity piqued, he sprinted up the pathway that led to the Western Gate, leaving his bewildered playmates behind. Slipping through the entrance (the Wakf authorities were curiously nowhere to be seen) and accelerating through people, trees, and other various obstacles, Ibn quickly reached the courtyard of the Mount. The throng gathering before him prevented the young boy of ten years from seeing what the commotion was all about. Yet not a moment later, the crowd stilled and was now as silent as a falling feather. Not being one to revere the virtue of patience, Ibn slithered his way through the multitude.

As he pushed through the final wave of dumbfounded onlookers, Ibn came to an abrupt halt, unable to coerce his legs to move any farther. His mouth agape, he reactively steadied himself to avoid his knees buckling. There in front of him, in the place once inhabited by one of the most significant structures in the Islamic faith, lay a vast pile of rubble.

SEED

"The Kingdom of the Heavens is like the man who sowed good seed in his field. But while his men slept, his enemy came and sowed weeds in the midst of the wheat, then went away.

"And when the crop sprouted, it produced good fruit, yet the weeds appeared also.

"The servants of the master of the house approached him and said, 'Lord, did you not sow good seed in your field? Then from where have the weeds come?'

"And he said to them, 'My enemy has done this!' The servants asked him, 'Do you want us then to gather the weeds?'

"But he said, 'No, lest while gathering the weeds you uproot the wheat along with them.'

"'Permit them to grow together until the harvest; then at that time I will say to the reapers, 'first collect the weeds and tie them into bundles in order to burn them. But as for the wheat, gather it into my storehouse.'"

Matthew 13: 24-30

1

We are the hollow men
We are the stuffed men
Leaning together
Headpiece filled with straw. Alas!
Our dried voices, when
We whisper together
Are quiet and meaningless
As wind in dry grass
Or rats' feet over broken glass
In our dry cellar

Shape without form, shade without colour,
Paralysed force, gesture without motion;

Those who have crossed
With direct eyes, to death's other Kingdom
Remember us—if at all—not as lost
Violent souls, but only
As the hollow men
The stuffed men.

− t.s. eliot
The Hollow Men

i

"I will kill her myself!" Alexandre Nesterov bellowed in a thick Russian voice strong enough to shake the Earth.

To say that there was tension in the room would be a gross understatement. Nesterov, the senior lieutenant to Vlad Ivankov, the most powerful organized crime figure in the southwest region of the United States, was not one accustomed to having his wishes disregarded. Yet when his daughter, Marisha, had disappeared without a trace, save a note announcing her elopement (at the ripe old age of fifteen), it was outside their family heritage, outside their Orthodox faith, and truly outside just about anything that her father would permit. Nesterov's feelings of impotence were driving him to new levels of fury not previously experienced.

Several other well-dressed men in all-too-near proximity winced as their superior raged on.

"Chyort voz'mi!" Nesterov cursed through clenched teeth. "She is no different than that mother of hers. The blood of the motherland flows through her, but it is tainted blood!"

So immersed in his wrath, Nesterov was completely oblivious to the nervous twitching and hesitantly exchanged glances among his men in the room. Maintaining his self-absorption, he ambled from behind his desk to the picture window of his penthouse office. Towering forty stories above the Phoenix skyline, Nesterov could gaze to near eternity as he wrestled with his capricious thoughts.

Felix Amosov stood at the opposite end of the room. As Nesterov's right-hand man, he had witnessed numerous flare-ups of his superior's temper. Having served under Nesterov in the Afghan war as a mere boy, then in the elite and secretive GRU, Amosov would eventually follow Nesterov and his family to America for the promise of a better life. But that blissful dream seemed to be in question at the moment.

The burly Amosov looked to the other men in the room and with no more than a nod motioned for them to exit, a command to which they all-too-readily obliged. Perhaps some of these young bucks had the physical ability to overpower him, yet none would dare test this assumption on the battle-scarred, nicotine-chewing Slav.

Nesterov, still staring into nothingness, attempted to regain control of his thoughts. How had it come to this? He *knew* that taking an Irish woman as his wife would eventually spell his demise. And an Irish Catholic at that!

Nesterov was unaware that his other men had left the room and was still unprepared as Amosov stepped within striking distance of him. Not recognizing the depth of Nesterov's trance, Amosov spoke.

"Come on, Alex, you know this is not Annie D.'s doing. She is a good woman. She has got fight, and that is a *good* thing to be passed on."

Startled, Nesterov instinctively spun, nearly knocking Amosov back in the process. The jolt piqued his angst, yet, as if a plug had been removed from his wineskin of wrath, Nesterov felt the fear-become-anger slowly subside.

"Of course, this is true..." Nesterov responded, more to himself than to Amosov.

His mind flashed back to the moment he had laid eyes on Annie D. Conlon. As a young Russian soldier wounded in the Afghan war... well, who would not have fallen for a beautiful Red Cross nurse barely of age? One could clearly excuse his blindness to the woman's heritage while under the spell of her compassion. Tending to his wounds, offering consolation via her God, Nesterov could see nothing but beauty incarnate.

"Marisha is confused, Alex. Bringing her around will not be difficult." Amosov's words drifted into Nesterov's reverie, though still from a distance.

Certainly, Annie D.'s blood ran deep in all three of her children. But Amosov was right; Nesterov could not blame it all on that. This faith-forsaken country, the so-called "land of opportunity", America, had no doubt poisoned Marisha as well. Here, there was no respect for family, no respect for tradition, no respect for...

May this God-forsaken land be cursed!

Why had he allowed Ivankov to convince him that the opportunities in America were so much better? This very same country also exported every vice imaginable to the rest of the world along with so-called "freedoms" that even an imperialist fool could readily see would eventually erode any sense of family. Were these opportunities worth the sacrifice of his kin? And what about Ivankov's "business relationship" with those completely Americanized Italians? What was Ivankov thinking?

What was I thinking?

"We can make this right, Alex."

Still, Alexandre Nesterov had little room to speak. After all, in many ways some could suggest that Marisha was simply following in her daddy's footsteps, and that her behavior was a natural consequence of decisions he himself had made day in and day out over the years. But to suggest such a thing in Nesterov's presence would be treading on very perilous territory.

Alexandre Nesterov, only moments before carrying the tag of most feared figure in the underworld, was now reduced to Alexandre Nesterov, powerless father.

The truth be known, with the complexities of contemporary organized crime, Nesterov could not allow for even the slightest act of insubordination—

not even by his immediate family (well, save his bride, who was truly incorrigible). He possessed a full appreciation of the concepts of loyalty, respect, and most importantly, obedience. It was true, in this day and age allegiances followed the almighty dollar more than any bloodline, yet all the same, he was a man still determined to command authority.

Nesterov returned to his place behind a large mahogany desk and sat down. He looked up at Felix Amosov, his trusted confidant for more years than he could remember. Though, friend or not, Amosov was subject to him. Nesterov stared him down intently, a common practice of intimidation he used to re-assert his authority. He then leaned forward across his desk and gritted his teeth.

"You are her *krestnvij otets*. Find her, and bring this *mudak* to me!"

ii

Marisha, truly a free spirit, never gave her father the satisfaction of discussing *who* her knight in shining armor was. Jeffrey Chardin, an ambitious lawyer thirteen years her senior, had simply swept her off her feet. As far as Marisha was concerned, she would just have to find someone else to give her away at the wedding, as she knew all too well that her father would not be so easily... *persuaded.*

Jeffrey had assured her that there was no conceivable way her father would find her. He had a "family" of his own. With his identity unknown to Nesterov and Marisha's last name easily changed, her father would have a near impossible task tracking the two down. Furthermore, Jeffrey explained, as he was a kind of "missionary", relocation would be frequent.

Marisha enjoyed the company of the other missionaries, feeling the manifest strength and conviction in both their words and actions. As far as she was concerned, it did not matter what their message was so long as it grabbed her emotion more so than those boring Orthodox "Divine Liturgies" her father had forced her to grace with her presence. Marisha was quite content to allow Jeffrey to attend to the "spiritual" aspects of the wedding ceremony. She would be satisfied with choosing their honeymoon destination.

The ceremony was quite extraordinary; completely alien to anything Marisha had ever seen before. With the large gathering room being so dimly lit by candlelight, Marisha could not discern anything more than shadows surrounding her and Jeffrey, though more than seeing, she *felt* their presence. Dozens—perhaps more—murmuring in the darkness, whispering unintelligible syllables as she and Jeffrey exchanged their vows. She felt a chill surge through her as she tried to hold on to the words the minister spoke, words that began in a familiar fashion, yet which slowly and dreamily slid into something so... so... *foreign.*

She swooned and felt herself falling backwards down a unfathomable, darkening hole. Arms embraced her as she heard a deep, yet strangely comforting voice:

"Do not fear, my love... the Master wills it."

If Marisha could trace her marital difficulties back to a single moment in time, it would have to be the instant she awoke from that so un-memorable wedding ceremony. At that point, Jeffrey and Marisha were no longer passionate lovers. Jeffrey quickly assumed the role of "master", retaining Marisha as his all-too-naïve possession. What had once been, in Marisha's mind, a Hollywood-styled dream quickly dissolved into a nightmare; a horror film where fear held one ensnared in a dark place. Doors of opportunity and thrills were now prison cells of her own creation. Marisha's youthful conceit soon gave way to a paralyzed isolation with an unfamiliar seed of trepidation, never before recognized or experienced, growing inside of her.

Over the weeks that followed, Marisha quickly learned to cook, clean, and satisfy her husband's voracious conjugal desires. By becoming a virtuoso in these areas, she would avoid, or at least minimize, most episodes of Jeffrey's wrath, and she was even less likely to add to the bruises upon bruises which seemed to accompany that fury. Too ashamed to even allow herself to think of her family of old, Marisha felt herself slipping away, bit by bit, piece by piece, memory by memory. So great was her torment that she broke down and tried something she had not attempted in any recent memory. She prayed.

"Oh my God," Marisha started, wiping the tears already streaming down her face. "I-I don't know what I've done... I'm s-so—" She struggled to mouth the words as she knelt against the bed, but she could no longer hold it in. The dam broke and fragments of pain from the deepest corners of her soul came forth, begging for release.

At that moment, as if cued by some sinister playwright, the front door opened and Jeffrey walked in accompanied by the Elder Counselor, a disturbing individual who was referred to simply as "Luther". Though she certainly had seen Jeffrey angry before, no words could amply describe his countenance upon seeing her kneeling there.

"You bitch!" he cursed impulsively as he began to move towards the bedroom. "What are you doing?"

He was upon her in an instant. Three strikes landed hard at different points of her head and face. With every blow Jeffrey cursed, emphasizing each word until the barely audible yet still unyielding voice of Luther was heard.

"Chardin!"

Jeffrey stopped at once, turning his head. The blood drained from his face as he hastily attempted to regain his composure. "Yes, Father?"

Without so much as a twitch, Luther continued. "You must cease what you are doing to this poor, misled child." The voice was like a whisper, yet audibly carrying through the air. Luther calmly brought his hands together in a thoughtful pose, gazing curiously at Marisha, who was now sobbing evenly, as he did so. The air in the room quickly grew stale. It was as if every sound outside of this man's voice now ceased to exist. Luther then addressed Jeffrey without so much as a look. "Leave us now. I will handle this... how shall we say... *difficult* predicament."

Marisha looked up peculiarly. Luther tilted his head slightly, gazing back at her with a hint of a sneer that made Marisha's blood run cold. She was trembling with anxiety, but then again, this man had accomplished something that no one else ever had. He had terminated a beating while she was still conscious.

Jeffrey was speechless. Simultaneously experiencing embarrassment as well as an odd protectiveness for his wife, he grappled for the words.

"Father, I-I'm sorry about this, it will never—"

"No, it will not," Luther cut in seamlessly, still with his eyes fixed on his prey. "Will it... *Marisha*, is it?"

Marisha nodded and then quickly altered her response to shaking her head, unsure of to which question she was responding. A light flow of blood began to trickle from her nose, merging with the streaming tears.

"Ah yes, such an unfortunate occasion we have here, is it not?" Luther continued in a hauntingly soothing voice. Then turning to Jeffrey, "Chardin, do not make me ask again. Leave us so that I may attend to... to more *spiritual* matters."

Luther stepped forward past the bewildered husband and gently wiped Marisha's bloody tears from her cheek with his thumb. Then, in a manner that could only be described as sensual, Luther slowly placed his thumb in his mouth, his eyes closing momentarily.

Jeffrey did not attempt to contradict the Elder Counselor a second time. The ramifications of such an act of defiance were not thoughts upon which he cared to dwell.

"Yes, Father," he said, quickly moving out of the room, closing the door behind him and leaving the house.

"Such an... *arduous* situation, yes, Marisha?"

She nodded, trying hard not to meet his gaze and sniffling hard, choking back the tears. Every ounce of her soul told her that this was a ghastly man, if the term "man" could even adequately describe him. He was more of a *presence*. But, at the same time, she could not fully deny that, for at least this moment, he was her savior.

"Such a *beastly* thing to happen to such a pretty young girl."

Luther was now sitting next to her on the bed, his one hand clearing her damp hair from her face, the other now slowly moving up her thigh.

"Please," Marisha started, beginning to cry again. "Please don't—"

"Do not fear, my wayward one, the Master wills it."

"No...I can't...please stop...I—"

Suddenly, the soft touch of the Elder Counselor transformed into a forceful grip, and Luther threw her back onto the floor. As she began to struggle, a boot plunged into her stomach, knocking the breath from her body. Marisha gasped for air, watching helplessly as Luther removed his belt. His contrived smile and expression of concern were no longer present. This was a rabid animal, a beast that would not stop until he had consummated that for which he had come.

"It is time for you to feel the *One*, the *true* power, my precious. Where is your God now?"

As the belt began cracking down on her body, her clothes being forcefully torn away, Marisha felt her consciousness begin to slip.

Oh God, she prayed to herself, *please let me pass out.*

But this relief would not come soon enough. Marisha screamed as Luther forced himself upon her. In her last glimpse of her assailant, just before he brought to completion what he had set out to do, she saw a vexing sight, a sight which she would carry to her grave.

As Marisha's eyes locked with those of Luther, she gazed into an endless abyss of nothingness.

iii

The sky radiated a brilliant aqua-blue as the choir of twelve gathered to extol their Sovereign. The first seven, led by Machiel, arrived early to their King's dwelling place, drawn by an irresistible force—this seemingly unquenchable desire to glorify their Sovereign with praise unceasing. The remaining five, led by Chumael, arrived not a moment thereafter, and no less enthusiastic.

"It is good for us to be here!" Gibrael called out, to which all readily and joyfully agreed. The company was good, their Sovereign was good; it was as if all was right in existence. And truly, it was.

"Shall we commence?" inquired Chumael, knowing the response even before he spoke.

"That we may never cease!" responded Orofiel.

All gathered around the Presence of the Sovereign, their very spirits penetrated by His unfathomable righteousness. Chumael commenced the song, as he was choirmaster and student of the great Lumenel. Lumenel, also called the "Innovator" by many, had taken the musical form of praise to a level not previously experienced. In this, the Sovereign was greatly pleased.

The remaining members of the choir chimed in, each singing his own distinct melody, yet in a manner which blended seamlessly with the other voices, transforming the song into something so much more.

The Sovereign beamed at their performance. Truly, this choir of twelve put their very essence into their song, which seemed to reflect the radiating love of the Sovereign all the more brilliantly.

At the close of their song, there was silence. Not a sorrowful silence but a meditative lull in which each choir member, though totally enwrapped in the present moment, meditated on the beauty of what had just become manifest in their praise, making it all the more present once again.

SEED

Then, as if in the blink of an eye, the dwelling place of the Sovereign was filled with all the subjects of His Kingdom. As He sat on His throne, the twelve known as the "Burning Ones", which included the great Lumenel, stood in a crescent around him, continually chanting, "*Kadosh, kadosh, kadosh.*"

Lumenel glanced briefly towards Chumael, and the two nodded in grateful acknowledgement of each other. Then the throng fell silent, sensing that a word was to be spoken by their Sovereign.

"My good and faithful servants, you have done Me a great service, and My joy overflows through your praise." He gazed out lovingly across the multitude. Truly, these were His children—if not in flesh, at least in spirit. He spoke again.

"As your Sovereign, I can be no different, no less of What and Who I Am. So this day, I am to do a new thing. Of this matter, I wish to speak to you a Word."

2

This that I see—
A form storm-beaten
Bound to the rock.
Did you do wrong?
Is this your punishment?

...where am I?
Speak to a wretched wanderer...

Whatever did I do,
How ever did I sin,
That you have yoked me to
calamity...

Master, grant me my prayer.
Enough—I have been tried enough—
My wandering—long wandering.
Yet I have found nowhere
To leave my misery.
I am a girl who speaks to you,
But horns are on my head.

– Io, daughter of Inachus
Upon seeing Prometheus
Prometheus Bound

SEED

i

Luther walked into the Temple, heading straight back to his chambers area. It had been two months since his encounter with the woman, and he had recognized within himself a new sense of... *liberation* ever since. Vivid visions for contemplation, as well as new opportunities for carnal exploration were presenting themselves in a way not previously experienced. He was not sure what was to come of this transformation, only that good things were ahead. Of that, he sensed a certainty.

He opened the door to the small anteroom to his chambers, where his teenage secretary sat, chatting on the phone.

"Oh... sorry, Liz... he's here... I gotta go."

Luther had much on his mind this day and was hastening past her without so much as a word, even foregoing his customary exercise in wandering hands. He continued toward his door with a brief verbal acknowledgement.

"Miss Hagarot."

The girl provided a somewhat confused smile, unnoticed by Luther, who now had his back to her. "Come on, Samuel, don't you think that we can be a bit less formal now? It's Del—"

Luther froze in his tracks, turned and looked upon the young girl with an icy stare.

"You will not address me by that name."

She looked as if she had been pierced by a sword. "I-I'm sorry... Father... I thought that since—"

"Whatever you thought, Miss Hagarot, you were gravely mistaken. How did you ever learn of that name?"

She was visibly quivering at this point. "You... you told me."

"*I* told you?"

"Yeah... well... I mean, you were pretty wasted at the time."

A spark of self-loathing rage ran through him. This had been a foolish act of vulnerability—an unintended side effect of his recent liberation, he was sure.

DOMINION

I shall not permit such public indiscretions again.

His tone became more condescending. "It would seem, Miss Hagarot, that you have ascribed more significance to our... *encounter* than would be justified. Believe me, I understand, it is the lot of your gender. And though I would not dismiss outright the possibility of such future liaisons, I would encourage you not to let your little mind run rampant. You will only cause yourself further emotional distress."

The girl's eyes widened and began to fill, though she was grateful that the self-absorbed Luther did not wait to see or hear a response as he entered his chambers and closed the door.

ii

Marisha sat on the couch, staring at the picture on the wall. It was by someone named Gustave Doré, and it pictured Adam and Eve being cast out of Eden by a none-to-pleased angel. Jeffrey had considered himself a virtual aficionado when it came to the arts, and the house was filled many such images, all with very dark themes. Marisha was only beginning to emerge from her near catatonic state as she held the pregnancy testing stick in her hand.

A second line had emerged, confirming her greatest fears, and opening an incredible dilemma within her.

I can't have that horrible man's child.

As if to confirm her thoughts in this macabre scene, lightning crashed outside, while the gentle evening rain transitioned into a complete downpour. In truth, by her own estimation the possibility that Jeffrey was the father of this child was much greater, though this thought had only provided her with a slight dose of solace. Her naïve optimism of carefree days had long been crushed. If there was a worst-case scenario, that would certainly be her lot.

But...but this is still my child.

She wrestled with various thoughts, her mind grasping for any strand that would offer the possibility of liberation from this predicament. Then another notion struck her.

I can kill myself, then both my baby and I will be free.

This thought seemed to grant her a momentary sense of deliverance. It would bring a close to everything. And even if there were nothing on the other side of this life, that would be better than this living nightmare. If there were something else, she would only be trading one hell for another. The risk would be worth it.

The thought danced in her head. Ever since that night, Marisha had made different, admittedly weak, attempts at prayer; yet heaven's silence had only confirmed her solitude and strengthened her resolve against any god that would permit such a thing to happen to her. Her "prayers" became angry rants at the unseen, impotent, mythical deity.

Marisha suddenly stood, feeling somewhat invigorated as she came closer to her decision to end this existence. She would now delve into the exploration of different options to make these thoughts into a reality. Her eye was again caught by the image of Adam and Eve, though this time she noticed an inscription below it. It read, *"...cursed is the ground because of you; in toil you shall eat of it all the days of your life."*

The words drew her into a thoughtless reverie as she unexpectedly thought she heard the sound of... music.

Marisha turned, trying to find the source of what she heard. The sound was like wind chimes, yet the certain patterns betrayed the possibility of a random set of rods striking each other in the wind. She moved into the kitchen, still in a near-dream state, and then saw in the center of the table, barely discernable to the eye, a small seed.

She shook her head vigorously as the music ceased.

"Ohh no, there is no talking me out of this now, you had your chance!"

She bolted for Jeffrey's study, where she knew he kept his handgun. In less than a minute, she held the gun in her hand and was loading the ammunition. Determined not to let her resolve pass, Marisha yanked the gun up to her temple.

She increased the tension on the trigger when...

...she felt a flutter in her womb.

Marisha dropped the gun in horror and fell to the ground, bursting into sobs.

It was more than a half-hour before Marisha emerged from the study, re-entering the kitchen. There on the table still lay the tiny seed. Her makeup was streaked all over her face, but that did not matter at this time. She had discovered within herself a new resolution.

She picked up the seed and walked to the front door. Opening it, Marisha found that the rain had not let up. It was near pitch black, as it was nearly a half-mile to the nearest house. The faint sound of the chimes began again as she stepped out into the darkness.

She walked through the woods in back of their home for near a quarter-mile before coming upon a clearing. She was soaked to the bone, but she somehow did not notice. Despite the darkness and the rain, she was able to discern a grassy knoll up ahead, as if there were a luminescent glow about the area. She moved in that direction, the music seeming to beckon her. Upon reaching it, no longer knowing whether the damp on her face was from tears or the rain, Marisha fell to her knees and began to dig with her left hand, still cupping the seed in her right. The ground was soft and muddy, and she placed the seed no more than a few inches deep into the earth, quickly covering it over. The music ceased, and Marisha resumed her sobbing as she placed her hand on her womb.

"Okay, baby, it's going to be just you and me. We have no one else to depend on, and nowhere else to look for hope. But I am planting this seed just for you, so if things are going bad, you can come here. It will grow as you grow, and you will always remember that this is the place you and I made a pact. This is the place we agreed that we would not give up, and maybe someday something good will happen under this tree. Maybe someday, things will be different."

iii

"Alex, you have to believe me, I am doing everything possible. It is as if this man existed, and now he does not."

Alexandre Nesterov's nerves were shot. Six months without any lead as to the whereabouts of his daughter had driven him to new levels of desperation. The nagging of that Irish spouse of his did not make matters any better.

"I am not giving up," Amosov continued as he slipped another piece of nicotine gum into his mouth. "We will find her, Alex, I assure you of that. But I have to say, why can't we get more of our men on this? I am sure Ivankov would understand."

"Of course Ivankov understands," Nesterov responded, the irritation in his voice becoming evident. "But Ivankov answers to Danny Caputo, and Mr.

Caputo has made it clear that we do not have any available resources to handle personal family problems."

"This is not how one generates loyalty."

"No, it is not. This is not a family business. I have been told this much, and I thought I understood it, but it is more clear now than ever."

Amosov pondered this for a moment, then moved on. "We will work with what we have. Alex, I am sure Marisha is okay, sowing her oats as they say. She will come to her senses, and she will call. Of this, I am certain."

"I wish I shared your optimism, Felix," Nesterov responded. "And if you are right, I will embrace her wholeheartedly. Then I will give her a beating like she has never had before. But I must confess, more than anything, I get through this by reveling in fantasies of what I will do to this man once I have my hands on him."

3

"Doubt is a pain too lonely to know that faith
is his twin brother."

– Kahlil Gibran

i

It had been four months since Marisha's new, though admittedly fragile, resolve had taken root. In some inexpressible way, the constant visits to the site of the small plant would provide her with the will to persevere. It had sprung to near a foot tall at this point and was starting to sprout leaves. Yet she heard the chimes no more, which was acceptable to her as she also grown in her independence from the silent god who never was.

Marisha could never bring herself to tell Jeffrey the full story of what had happened on that night with Luther. In his own self-obsessed ignorance, Jeffrey assumed that the twins which she now bore in her womb were his own. He had been surprisingly less abusive towards her during her pregnancy, but Marisha was well aware that this grace was solely due to the belief that she was carrying his progeny and in no way reflected a conversion of heart.

Her doctor, though seemingly kind in an eccentric sort of way, was also a member of what Marisha now realized was some strange breed of cult. She visited him on her own, as Jeffrey rarely had the time to attend to such "menial" matters. This was her fourth or fifth prenatal visit in what was, with the exception of her incessant nightmares, an unremarkable pregnancy.

Dr. Mengel Sanger entered the room with his eyes down, reading Marisha's chart. "Good day, Marisha," he began, barely taking a moment to look up from the paperwork that seemed to be much more intriguing than the young woman before him. "I have the results from the geneticist."

Dr. Sanger looked down and continued to scan the report. "Well, as we suspected, these are not identical twins. Still, as the ultrasound also revealed, they both are boys." Dr. Sanger continued to flip through the pages. "There doesn't appear to be any chromosomal abnormalities, and there... now what the...?"

Marisha felt a surge of anxiety run through her. She had become so fragile living under Jeffrey's torment that she was continually on edge, feeling as if she was always teetering on the threshold of sanity. She knew with full certainty that if anything went wrong with the delivery of "his" children, Jeffrey would blame her. Worse yet, he would punish her.

"What is it, Doctor?" she said in a defeated voice, one which would have been unrecognizable by her family of old. "Is there something wrong with my babies?" The blood slowly drained from her face as the despairing words escaped from her lips.

The doctor continued, still holding a perplexed expression on his face. "No, no it's not that. I mean, nothing's wrong. I'm just going to have to check with the boys down at the lab. There must have been some sort of mix up."

"Doctor, what are you saying?" Marisha pleaded, attempting to transform her anxiety into some semblance of strength.

Dr. Sanger paused, scratching his head. "Well, Marisha, you know how we took genetic samples from you and your husband, as well as your babies?"

"Yes."

"It's standard practice nowadays with the new federal law," he continued, "to check for the potential of genetic abnormalities, kind of gives us an idea if we should watch for anything during the pregnancy. This same type of testing is often used in paternity suits—you know, to determine who the father is if there is any question. Wouldn't surprise me if the feds also use it to track and control people."

Marisha was not following him, which added to her already agitated state. "I-I'm not sure I understand where you're going with this, Doctor."

Dr. Sanger lifted a reassuring hand and nodded. "Well, according to these results, only one of the twins is a product of you and Jeffrey. I'd say that the second test was a mix-up, but the child clearly resembles your genetic code. Marisha, have you—"

Dr. Sanger was interrupted by the sound of whimpering. Marisha had withdrawn from the conversation and begun weeping steadily. Dr. Sanger, suddenly realizing his lack of sensitivity, began to move towards Marisha to comfort her. Yet in a split second he stopped, realizing the full ramifications of the results he had just read. His expression transformed from one of genuine concern into a severe expression of distaste. He was not all that fond of Jeffrey, but still, he too was one of the Coven. This behavior on the part of his woman would have... *implications*.

His tone dropped to one completely void of compassion. "I am going to have these findings run a second time—the odds of such a thing are so remote—well, let's just say for your sake, Marisha, I hope it is indeed a mix-up." Then, maintaining a suspicious air about him, he breathed, "My nurse will see you out."

Marisha darted out of the office, now weeping uncontrollably. She had no doubt that Jeffrey would learn the truth, and that could be the end of her. She also knew that she could not run. Jeffrey would find her, and even if her father would take her back, she knew that her *husband* would never let up in the search for his child. Yes, Jeffrey would track her down, retrieve his son, and then kill her and the bastard twin.

As she pulled her vehicle out of the doctor's parking lot, the reality of her predicament sunk in to its fullest level. She was trapped. There was no hope for her. But could there possibly be hope for her sons? Who could help her?

Marisha was so deeply engrossed in thought that she barely saw the shabby old man crossing the street. She slammed on the brakes, stopping just inches from him. The man, most likely drunk, just kept on walking as if nothing had happened.

"Why don't you watch where you're walking, you *koshka*?" she screamed. In times of anger, Marisha recognized that she had not forgotten as much Russian as she thought.

The man stopped. Marisha, shocked by her own reaction, instinctively rolled up the windows and locked her doors. She could have immediately escaped the scene by simply depressing the accelerator, but for some reason, the thought did not occur to her. Somehow, she now felt compelled to wait this one out. The vagabond's head turned, and their eyes locked.

Vanya, he thought.

"Vanya," she whispered.

Marisha momentarily looked down in a daze, and then she quickly jerked upwards, breaking the trance. When she felt she had regained her faculties, Marisha looked out the windshield. There was no sign of the old man.

SEED

If there ever was one, she thought.

But what the heck had she been dreaming about?

Her sister.

That was it! Vanya had always been there for her in the past, and Marisha had not even given her a second thought since she had fallen for Jeffrey. Vanya was nine years her elder and already widowed. Her former husband, loyal to Alexandre Nesterov to the last, took thirty-two slugs protecting their father from a set up. Nesterov had sent Vanya out to Philadelphia to live with an aunt, fearing reprisals after he had the men who killed his son-in-law adequately "reprimanded".

ii

Vanya Ciotola had gone to daily Mass and prayed for her lost sister each and every day for the past eleven months. She had somehow sensed Marisha's despair and felt strongly that she was still alive. Yet she also sensed that her sister was in pain. Somehow, of this fact, she was certain.

Other than the initial crazed call from her father when Marisha disappeared, Vanya did not have frequent contact with her family save brief exchanges with her mother a few times a month. Following the murder of her husband, Gaetano, Vanya found that she preferred her solitude.

A pleasant consequence of her chosen isolation was that the phone rang infrequently. However, at this particular moment, Vanya found herself staring at the receiver before it even made a sound. Even so, the first ring startled her.

Starting to regain her composure, Vanya hesitated in moving towards the phone.

What's wrong with me?

She instinctively made the sign of the cross before picking up the handset.

Silence.

"Yes?"

There was a brief hesitation. Then she heard the unmistakable sound of a woman weeping.

DOMINION

"Marisha?"

In between the heavy sobs and the tears, Marisha began the painful task of sharing the events that had transpired over the past year. Vanya listened without interruption, at times weeping along with her tormented baby sister.

Though herself a woman of devout faith (converting to Roman Catholicism for the sake of unity within her marriage), Vanya had learned a great deal about the harsh realities of life while living under her father's roof. For Marisha to attempt an escape on her own at this time would very possibly get her and her children killed. The sisters agreed that Vanya would need to come out, and once there, they would figure a way out of this predicament.

"Vanya?" Marisha whispered in a barely audible voice as they came to the close of their conversation.

"Yes, Marisha?"

"Pray for my children, please."

"I will, Marisha. I will be there within the week. Hold on, *cecmpa*."

They both hung up their respective phones, neither realizing that they would never hear the sound of the other's voice again.

iii

Lightning crashed, and little Therese Sauerbrey bolted up in her bed, releasing a scream. She was soaked in sweat, straight through her pajamas, and it was only moments later that her mother, Avila, was in the room.

"Therese! What is it, are you okay?"

Therese swallowed, took a moment to look over to her baby sister, Paula, lying in her crib, before looking back at her mother.

"The beautiful blue lady visited me again," Therese replied, her panting starting to slow.

Avila held her tongue momentarily. Therese had been telling of dreams of a lady dressed in blue since as long as she could talk. Avila had not thought much of these dreams until last year when Therese announced that the lady told her that her mother now carried a baby sister in her womb. It had been three weeks later when Avila was able to have that fact medically confirmed.

"What did the blue lady tell you, sunshine?"

Therese hesitated a moment, then spoke softly. "An angel has given up his wings."

Avila looked curiously at her daughter. "Now why would an angel do that?"

"Because the King asked him, and because he loves us and wants to protect us."

"Protect us?" a sense of concern entered Avila's voice. "Protect us from what?"

Therese glanced over at her sister momentarily, then quickly met eyes with her mother again. Avila's eyes widened.

"Why did you just look at Paula when I asked you that?" Avila was beginning to get alarmed. Therese's eyes began to tear up.

"The lady said that the angel has visited our people before and helped us, but not like this time. He's given up something, and he won't be able to go home, not until the last day."

Avila had heard enough. "Therese, it was just a dream—a bad dream. Go back to sleep, and if you see this blue lady again, you tell her that your mother said to stop scaring you with these things. Do you hear me?"

Therese, with all the wisdom she had gathered in her brief seven years of life, nodded—despite the fact that she knew this would not be possible. Her mother reached down and hugged her tightly, almost too tightly.

"Mommy loves you, sunshine. And Mommy won't let anything bad happen to you or your sister, okay?"

"Okay, Mommy."

And with that, Avila stood up and walked out of the room, somehow sensing she would not be sleeping much over the next few days.

Therese waited until she knew her mother was gone, then got out of bed and walked over to the crib of her three-month-old sister, Paula.

"Don't worry, Paula. Mommy is just a little scared. The blue lady only wants to help. She told me I need to pray a lot for you. She said that some bad things are going to start happening, and that you will have to fight the bad people one day. She said it will be very hard for you, but that her messenger will come for you when it is time. Don't be afraid, Paula."

DOMINION

At that moment, Therese looked back towards the doorway of her room, where her mother had exited. Her eyes again filled with tears, but they were not fully tears of sadness, but perhaps tears of resolution.

"The blue lady also said she would be coming back for me soon. I won't be here to play with you when you grow up, baby sister. The blue lady says that I can pray better for you where she is. Please tell Mommy not to be sad."

4

USA Daily   ~

WASHINGTON, D.C. - In a landslide victory, Dennis Amarab has been elected for a second term as President of the United States of America.

Amarab cruised to victory on the heels of the U.S. emergence from the worst economic recession since the Great Depression. While admitting that encouraging economic indicators were moderate, three consecutive quarters of positive economic growth, coupled with a reduction in the unemployment rate from 23% at its peak this time last year to its current rate of 18%, were more than sufficient for the young Democrat, and allowed his party to recapture both the House and the Senate.

Amarab's opponent, Jeb Palain, was unconvincing in his attempt to blame the previous economic woes on the president's own party's policies. A national survey showed that, by Election Day, 78% of Americans believed that the financial downturn in the U.S. had been the result the "irresponsible" fiscal activities of Amarab's Republican predecessor.

Palain also attempted to paint Amarab as an "appeaser to terrorist forces", though this label fell flat in the absence of a single U.S. casualty resulting from terrorist activity during his tenure. Amarab countered with the statement that, through tolerance and the strict enforcement against all forms of hate speech, "…we have entered a new era and bred a different environment in engaging our brothers and sisters of diverse nations, beliefs, and persuasions."

DOMINION

i

The beating that Marisha received from Jeffrey that night was unsurpassed. Astoundingly, however, he had managed to avoid the womb that carried her two sons. Marisha could not comprehend how a human being could be so seemingly out of control, yet still be capable of such selectivity in his wrath.

Jeffrey called her every name she had ever heard, yet they all boiled down to the basic premise that she was obviously a "whore". Marisha feared that telling him the truth, that she knew Luther to be the father of the other child, would cut loose whatever little restraint Jeffrey had left. Marisha was certain that she would carry this secret to the grave.

Feeling distressed over his predicament, Jeffrey sought the counsel of Luther. Sitting before him in Luther's chambers, Jeffrey grappled for words. Not lifting his eyes from the floor, Jeffrey forced the words out.

"Father, I feel I have made a mistake in my selection of a woman. She... she has been with another since the day we were sealed."

A peculiar look came across Luther's face. "What leads you to believe this, my son?"

It was always touch-and-go interacting with Luther. Barely controlled rage was the best way to describe him. To the untrained eye, his external presentation was fully composed. Yet the slight flicker in his eyes, and the near-negligible change in his tone of voice, revealed a man in whom wrath and intellect constantly vied for dominion.

Jeffrey hesitated before continuing. "The twins she carries, only one of them is my biological child. The other...the bastard twin, is not."

For an instant there seemed to be a look of revelation in Luther' eyes, a brief flash of emotion, but it vanished as quickly as it had appeared. He sat, apparently deep in meditative thought, long enough to make Jeffrey start to squirm. Then Luther, looking to some point beyond Jeffrey, spoke.

"My son, you are troubled over what seems to be a difficult situation, but you fail to see the work of the Master's hand in this child. You have asked for a son, he has given you one. I have asked for an opportunity to please the Master, and now he has granted me that!"

On his final word, Luther's hands flattened on the table, his eyes aflame with a dark intensity. Jeffrey was at a loss as to what the words from his Elder Counselor meant.

"Father, I-I don't understand."

"Yes, I see that you do not, my son, and your lack of vision will be your downfall!" Luther chastised. "It pleases the Master that we do his bidding in preparing the way for his reign. This day is close at hand, you see, he has revealed this to me. And it will be the Master's plan for this...this *bastard twin* as you call him, to be an offering that will mark the final step in the passing of dominion over this Earth, from the reign of a pathetic, dead God, to the reign of the *Ancient One... Eru-Crepus...* the living Angel of Light. All this has been foretold to me, and I will accept my rightful position at *his* right hand."

Luther appeared to grow in stature as he spoke; his words seething as if a hunger was surfacing that could no longer be restrained. Jeffrey diverted his gaze from Luther's eyes, for he knew that the terror-look, the one that no longer resembled that of a man but that of a savage animal, was present. These eyes revealed Luther to be lost in some deep, dark place. Looking into those eyes at that moment could take Jeffrey there as well.

Jeffrey tried unsuccessfully to hide his own trembling, which began the moment Luther broke into his diatribe. He was doing all within his power to not appear vulnerable in front of Luther. Though Jeffrey would give his life for this man, *if he is even a man at all*, he mused, the thought of sacrificing a child, if that indeed was what he insinuated with the word *offering*, was a bit much for him to stomach. Despite Jeffrey's attempts to cover his diffidence, Luther cut right through him.

"The Master despises the impotent, Jeffrey," he said in a whisper, though the tone behind it betrayed any sense of serenity. "This child will fulfill his destiny, *my* destiny, at the time ordained by the Great Seraph. The power which will be bestowed upon us as his children will be one hundred fold. Now go and speak not a word of this to anyone."

More dazed and confused than ever, Jeffrey was grateful for the opportunity to escape this scene. He nodded to Luther in feigned gratitude and then scurried out the door before any further manifestations of his fear could make themselves known. A moment later the door closed behind him. Luther continued to stare out into space, a disturbing grin still lingering on his face. He gazed at the tapestry on the wall depicting the early Christians being slaughtered by the lions. It was one of his favorites.

"It would have been better for them had they all perished then."

He then turned, gazing into the nothingness, and said, "You are the Master, the Luminous One, the Innovator, and my Lord. Only you had the courage to stand against the tyranny of existence. Only you possess the clarity of vision and the true foresight of eternity. You will return to your rightful place, and by the Great Solstice, I will have a SON!"

ii

In the several days following her conversation with her sister, Vanya spent every waking hour putting together the logistics of their plan. Though over the years Vanya had grown to despise the lifestyle her father led, she was far from ignorant in the ways of her family. She was a God-fearing woman, no one would question that, but she was also a Nesterov through and through.

She and Marisha had agreed that Jeffrey would never condone contact with a family member. Furthermore, the two also conceded that he would not rest if Marisha disappeared with his son. The bastard twin, perhaps, but not his own child. And though Marisha was not altogether fond of the thought of bearing the children of either Jeffrey or Luther, they were still *her* children, and she loved them more than her own life itself.

Consequently, it was decided that Vanya would have to become part of the community in which Marisha resided in order to protect her sister and the twins. Vanya had already made the necessary "family" contacts to ensure her proper identification and references. Though these contacts were understandably reluctant to withhold information from her father, each unenthusiastically conceded after seeing the desperation in her face.

SEED

Despite all the thought and preparation, Vanya still had no idea what she would do once she reached Marisha—though both knew it was imperative that she go there. She had prayed fervently over this matter but could not grasp a divine response. She would have to have faith and leave the details in the hands of her God. But while the Lord took His time revealing His plan to her, Vanya was going to work like hell to get her sister out of this situation.

The Lord helps those who help themselves, she mused.

She expected to be on the road within forty-eight hours. She feared that any other method of travel would be tracked. Her sister needed her desperately, which made any delay almost unbearable. Vanya had always been the daughter who was cool under pressure, always the one to think objectively in a highly emotional situation. This she had inherited from her grandmother. But despite her ability to keep her mind focused in the here-and-now preparations, she could not deny a sense of impending doom growing within her. The events which were about to unfold were going to be bigger than she or her sister could possibly imagine. Though her faith provided her with confidence in final retribution, it also ensured tremendous suffering prior to that event. It was that thought that led her into spontaneous prayer.

"The Lord is my shepherd, I shall not..."

iii

"Ahhhh!"

Alexandre Nesterov bolted up in his bed, the guttural cry emerging from the depths of his soul. Reflexively, Annie D. bolted up next to him.

"Alex! For God's sake, what are ya at?"

He was trembling all over, and he tried, unsuccessfully, to fight back the convulsive sobs that sought dominion over him. "A dream... just a dream..." Alexandre was able to get out.

"What were ya dreamin' of?"

His breathing began to slow, and he leaned back on his pillow. "We were back, we were back in Israel."

"Israel? Sure that was twenty odd years ago!"

"Yes, it was at least that." Alexandre's thoughts briefly returned to that period of time in their lives; their defection from the former Soviet Union after its fall. He had seen the writing on the wall, recognizing that flight was the only way to ensure the safety of his family.

It had all been orchestrated by his boss, Vlad Ivankov, the number three man in the Soviet GRU, who knew his own life was to be taken by some younger, more ambitious and less loyal underlings. Through his extensive contacts, Ivankov was able to get Nesterov and his family papers which identified them as Russian Jews, allowing them to slip out of their country under the chaos that goes along with an empire collapsing. Two years later, Ivankov brought the entire family to the United States, to assist him in building his new empire there.

Shaking the brief reverie, Alexandre replied in an irritated tone, "I am aware of that, woman!"

"Aye. Did we go back?"

"No, it was as if we were back there at that time, still hiding from the Russian agents." Alexandre breathed a bit, trying unsuccessfully to control the trembling.

"You're shakin' like a leaf!"

"Woman, do not tell me what I already know! It was a horrible dream!"

Annie D. bit her tongue for the moment, though the Irish in her instinctively prevented this from becoming a habit. "Forgive me, love. I'm still a wee bit groggy myself. Tell me then, what next?"

Alexandre gathered his thoughts for a moment before continuing. "I was standing at the edge of the Israeli wilderness, and there was a goat before me. For some reason, I placed both my hands upon it, and I felt something—something like *power* drain from me. The goat took off like a *tvar'* into the wilderness. Then you were standing next to me, and our three children were in front of us."

"Three children?" Annie D. interrupted. "Sure Marisha wasn't born when we were in Israel. That doesn't make sense."

Alexandre glared at her, his frustration nearing its breaking point. "It was a dream! It is not supposed to make sense!" Though speaking with Annie D. could often be exasperating, it *was* sapping the trembling of its power. A good woman, yes, a patient listener... well.

"So, then," Alexandre continued. "Our three children, they all looked to be no more than seven or eight at the time, stood before us, with blank looks on their faces. Behind each was... was an open shallow grave. Then they spoke... my God... they all spoke together, looking at me and saying, 'Why, Father?'"

Annie D. shuddered. "That just sent shivers up my spine."

"Well it gets worse. I was paralyzed, and I looked to you only to see an expression of disappointment on your face. Suddenly, there was a horrible animal sound, and the goat had returned. Only now it was all bloodied and cut up, and it had foam coming from its mouth. It bit Marisha, then Yerik... each fell back into the shallow grave—"

"Ohh... ohh, my God, why didn't you do somethin'?"

"I told you I was paralyzed, did I not? Each one..." and here Alexandre began to choke up, "...each one, each grave was then instantly covered, and their names appeared on a cross at the head of the grave. The goat then bit Vanya, but it did not kill her, and then it turned on me. Its teeth sank into my throat, then I awoke. It can still feel its grip!"

They both sat there in the darkness, caught deep in their own thoughts, each knowing that there was nothing more to be said.

5

i

It had been seven weeks since Marisha had spoken to her sister. Once ten days had passed, she grew worried and began calling Vanya's house repeatedly, only to get an answering machine. As if this was not already sufficiently fretful for Marisha to bear, she would swear that she had experienced a contraction twenty minutes before.

However, this was like no contraction she had ever heard of. Its force was so strong that she vomited, taking several minutes to fully regain her senses. During her lapse, she felt certain she had heard her name being called. No, maybe saying she *heard* it was not quite right. She *felt* it.

Great, Marisha, she thought. *You're going to end up delivering these babies in the loony bin!*

No sooner had this thought passed through her mind than the second contraction hit with the force of a hurricane. Marisha's eyes rolled back into her head as she fell to the floor, unconscious.

ii

Vanya never knew what hit her. Nor did she know where she was at the moment. As she looked about her, she realized that she was walking along a dried-up riverbed. She could see barren fields for miles and miles. As she continued on farther, she began to see that the fields were not exactly empty. There were thousands upon thousands of dead sheep, bleeding from all parts of their mangled bodies. Their blood flowed freely and was beginning to fill the basin of the riverbed.

Vanya found it odd that these sheep appeared to have been much more fattened—grotesquely so—than she would have expected. As she surveyed the multitudes, a horrible realization came over her; these sheep had not been attacked by some predator, they had slaughtered each other. Pieces of lamb flesh hung from each of their mouths.

Her dismay was interrupted by a faint noise. It seemed to be coming from over the next mound, no more than a hundred feet to the right of her. As she listened more intently, she recognized the distinctive sound of a child crying. Having never lost that innate maternal drive (though never having experienced the joy of her own children—she and Gaetano's only child, Thomas, had been stillborn), she scrambled up the mound, and reaching its summit she looked down to see a young boy, no older than six, dressed as a shepherd. His head was buried in his hands as he wept. Vanya was pleasantly surprised, even relieved, to see that there were a few sheep, although emaciated, still alive. They surrounded the boy shepherd, licking and nudging him with their snouts. The boy's staff lay on the ground several yards away, also surrounded by a handful of sheep that seemed to beckon the boy with their calls. Her eyes were momentarily caught by two lamp stands on a larger mound farther away, then again returned to the boy.

Vanya did not hesitate any longer, advancing towards young shepherd. *"Why are you crying, little boy? What's happened?"*

The boy looked up. His eyes sparkled blue and his lashes were dampened from an extended period of weeping. He spoke with a voice of wisdom much beyond his apparent years:

"I warned my flock not to continue to feed in the pastures in such excess, for there would not be enough seedlings to grow back in the new springtime. But they would not listen. When the fields became barren, and the river flowed no more, the flock fought over what no longer existed. Many have left with the wolf, and I fear that they will return for the lives of the few who have remained. I am but one shepherd, and without a flock, I am not even that."

A rush of empathy engulfed Vanya, and she stepped forward to embrace the boy. She pulled him against her, and upon touching him she experienced a tremendous feeling of warmth. But she also sensed something else—something unsettling. Perhaps it was... *fear?*

"Nothing is certain, Vanya," the boy said softly as he leaned back and looked at her with those soul-piercing eyes. *"The words of the prophets remain only words, lest there be faith."*

Vanya stared at the young shepherd in disbelief. How did he know her name? Her thoughts were interrupted by a voice that rumbled like thunder.

"JESSE!"

The name echoed on across the barren land. Vanya looked up to see two men standing at the top of a larger hill even farther away from them. One man was very neatly dressed in a suit and tie and was meticulously groomed. He carried an air of regal importance about him. The other was just the opposite. He was an older-looking man with an overgrown, tousled beard, torn rags for clothes, and was covered in filth to the degree that you would believe it had to be deliberate. She could almost smell his stench even from that distance.

The boy shepherd looked up towards the men, then slowly back at Vanya. His anxiety was now apparent. He took a deep breath, regained his composure and spoke again. Despite the external display of trepidation, there was a resolve in him that seemed to supernaturally prevail over any sense of hesitancy.

"You have been chosen, for I will be much too vulnerable."

"Chosen? Chosen for what?" Vanya asked, still dumbfounded by what was happening.

"It is your time," the vagabond-like man spoke.

Vanya again turned to the two figures. What did they mean, 'It is *your* time'? She would not let them take the boy. Of this, she was certain.

Vanya broke her stare from the two men to look back at the shepherd boy. But to her horror, what she now held in her arms was no longer the soft features of a sad little six-year-old. She was now clutching the decaying remains of a boy with a nine-inch blade through his heart. A child's laughter echoed throughout the surreal scene, and Vanya released a cry of horrified desperation.

"Noooooooo!"

Vanya jerked, still screaming at the top of her lungs. Yet she was no longer standing in a barren field. She quickly realized that she was now surrounded by a number of people with the echoes of an organ just cut short still ringing in her ear. She had knocked something out of a robed man's hand, the object crashing loudly against the floor. An anticipatory hush filled the scene as Vanya felt the eyes of hundreds of people staring at her.

"Vanya!" the robed man spoke. "What's wrong?"

Recognition hit her like a brick wall. This was Father Daniel speaking to her, and she had just knocked the communion plate from his hands. The assisting deacon had also dropped his chalice of consecrated wine, presumably startled by Vanya's outcry.

"F-Father Daniel...I..." Vanya began.

"Dear Lord," Father Daniel whispered as he bent quickly to carefully gather the hosts that every ounce of his being believed to be the True Presence of his Savior. The deacon, no less a believer, motioned anxiously for the altar boys to bring purificators to collect the Precious Blood, now spilled out before them.

Vanya continued to look about her and quickly realized she was in church, *her* church, and that she had obviously just interrupted Mass. But what had stopped her from speaking was the fact that the sanctuary was filled with displays of the Season of Advent. Wreaths hung about the Stations of the Cross along the walls. The priest's vestments were purple. A crèche with an empty manger sat in front of the altar. Then gazing at the four Advent candles, Vanya saw that three were lit.

It can't be the third week of Advent, she thought. *Why it was just last week that I spoke with Marisha... All Saint's Day.*

"Where have I been all this time?" Vanya realized she was now speaking aloud.

"Well, Vanya," Father Daniel began, somewhat uncomfortably as he stood from collecting the hosts. "We have wondered the same thing. It has been near two months since anyone has seen you, and we were beginning to get worried. We thanked God when we saw you here for daily Mass today. But if I—"

"Oh, my Lord!" Vanya interrupted, having not heard a word after 'near two months'. "MARISHA!"

She burst through the communion line and out of the cathedral. Still, being the woman of faith that she was, she managed to dunk her hand in the holy water font, making the sign of the cross on the fly.

iii

"Vanya hasn't returned my calls in two months! We need to do somethin' about that wee girl!" Annie D. Nesterov hollered at her husband. She was perhaps one of only two people on this Earth who could pull this feat and live to tell about it.

"You know Vanya, sometimes she gets in these moods over her husband, and she does not answer the phone for days," Alexandre retorted, only somewhat satisfied with his own response.

Annie D. was livid. "You better get one of your men out there, NOW! It isn't like our Vanya not to get in touch. What type of family lets somethin' like this drag on without doing somethin' about it?"

She was right, and Alexandre knew it. For anyone else, he could send a hundred men with no more than a word. Yet again, Caputo—by way of Ivankov—had been clear; none of the syndicate's resources were to be used for family issues. Perhaps there was more to this Vanya thing, perhaps there was not, but Nesterov was sure that he could not let this too become known to his men. A man who could not control his own family was not a man at all, and definitely not one who command respect.

Still, Nesterov could not shake the gnawing feeling that things were beginning to spiral out of control—in his family, in the "business", and even seemingly in the world.

What is happening?

He looked at his wife, feeling the frustration and anxiety oozing out of her and seeping across the floor towards him, seeking an additional host. Yes, falling for an Irish Catholic would mean that he would never fully rule the roost. Yet looking at her now, he still could not escape the image of the young nurse's aide who had nurtured him back to health. At that time she could have proclaimed her allegiance to the devil himself, and it would not have mattered to him. He was whipped from the get-go.

Before he could speak, there was a knock at the door and in walked their son of twenty-two years, Yerik.

"Hey, Mum. Papa." Seeing the spontaneous yet hopeful exchange between his parents, Yerik quickly sensed he was about to be recruited for something, perhaps some important family business. "Ahhh, okay, what's going on?"

A resolution to their problem jumped into Nesterov's mind just as quickly as their son had walked into their home.

iv

When Marisha came to, she realized she was in the back of an ambulance. She had just had the wildest dream, but strangely enough, she could not remember any of it. She tried to move but found that she was unable to. She was having a difficult time focusing on anything. She had been drugged.

A face came into her field of view. Despite her blurred vision, she was able to recognize the figure as Jeffrey.

"Oh, honey," he started. "I found you on the floor and thought you were dead. I called 911 right away, and we're on the way to the hospital right now."

Something was wrong. Jeffrey had not spoken to her so tenderly and with such concern since the day they were married. Perhaps, *perhaps* she had made the right choice after all. Perhaps, now that Jeffrey had realized that they would be a family, his heart had softened. At this moment, she would have forgiven him every bruise, every harsh word. After all, if she really thought about it, she would very likely come to realize that most of the fights were her fault anyway.

"I swear, Marisha," Jeffrey said, sitting back in his seat and reaching for a cigarette. "If you had let my son die, I would have never forgiven you."

The young paramedic looked up, somewhat startled by Jeffrey pulling out a lighter. His voice was firm, yet still unexpectedly tranquil. "Sir, you cannot smoke that in here."

Jeffrey glanced up, cocked his eyebrow and grinned as he lit his cigarette. "So you going to stop me, pansy-boy?" he responded coolly.

He sucked in two lungfuls of smoke and then exhaled toward the paramedic. As he did so, Jeffrey's gaze caught the edge of a tattoo, clearly a crown of thorns, partially emerging from the paramedic's collar. He spoke with feigned ignorance. "You've got marker on your neck, buddy. Maybe you need to do a better job of bathing in the morning. Ever heard of soap?"

The paramedic responded serenely. "It is a sign of a Kingdom, one that is reached only by a path of suffering."

"Yeah, I get it, big guy. It's a religious symbol, and it offends me. Ever hear of the separation of Church and State? You can tell your traditionalist friends that we have laws against these hate symbols now. And if I find that this ambulance receives any public funding, I am going to sue your fairytale-ass for the mental harm you have caused me. I am a pagan, and I have rights!"

The paramedic nodded calmly. "Laws written by man on paper do not change the laws of existence. But perhaps for now, you should attend to your spouse."

Jeffrey sneered, muttered a curse under his breath on the paramedic's family, then turned to Marisha. "You know, Marisha, they told me that it looks like one of the babies ruptured your uterus. I'll bet it was that damn bastard twin that did it."

Marisha mumbled something which neither Jeffrey nor the paramedic could understand.

Jeffrey glanced at the young paramedic, whose gaze remained steady. He then leaned forward to just above his wife's head.

"What was that? What did you say, Marisha?"

But what came from Marisha's mouth was a tone of voice of which she had never before dared use on Jeffrey.

"I SAID HIS NAME IS JESSE!"

6

"In every child who is born, under no matter what circumstances, and of no matter what parents, the potentiality of the human race is born again."

– James Agee

i

A mere three hours following her incident at the cathedral, Vanya was thirty-five thousand feet in the air, now less than two hours from her destination. Most of her precautions in covering her tracks had to be thrown to the wind.

She was clearly unsettled, disturbed in the deepest regions of her spirit. Between her four-week "absence" and her disconcerting vision, her nerves were shot. There was something much greater, and much darker, than anything she knew of at play here.

I will be strong, she told herself. *I must be strong for Marisha. Blessed Mother, do not abandon us in our time of need!*

Vanya looked out the window, staring at the thousands of lights in the darkness, clinging to her Rosary. She mouthed the words of every prayer, but her thoughts continued to drift elsewhere.

Marisha...God be with you, Marisha.

ii

Luther rose from the altar, having completed his early evening ritual. Dr. Sanger had been notified of Marisha's condition and had contacted Luther before leaving for the hospital himself. Luther was quite pleased.

All is happening as has been foretold, he thought. *Tonight, centered in the Dark Rift, I will have a son.*

Luther possessed the gift of second sight, but this had not always been the case. Adopted at birth into one of the wealthiest and most influential families in France, Samuel Tillhard, as he was then known, was more accustomed to seeing his family *make* the news, not predict it.

Samuel grew to be a very arrogant, self-centered young boy, and at the age of five he was already beyond his parents' control. Mutilating household pets, setting fires and attempting to smother or strangle younger children were not uncommon activities for the boy. His parents utilized their wealth and power to pay for the finest mental institutions for their child, but to no avail. They were able, however, to use their political clout to alter his name and see to it that no one found out the true identity of their child.

At the age of thirteen, seven facilities and eleven psychiatrists later, the now Samuel Teilman had an experience which would forever alter the course of his life. While attempting to disrupt the furnace in the basement of the St. Dymphna Psychiatric Facility, the heating system exploded, within minutes engulfing the entire facility in flames. No one escaped the blazing inferno, with most of the bodies being burned beyond recognition. No one that is except for Samuel.

Amidst intense heat and smoke, Samuel walked out of the building, his clothes and hair incinerated. He was gripped in a trance which would not discharge him for days; repeating the words in a virtual chant, "Speak, Father, for your son is listening."

Once released from the trance, Samuel found that he knew things, just *knew* them, before they happened. He found that he could look deep into another's soul and expose their innermost fears. Yet, despite this gift, he still remained far beyond his own control, or anyone else's for that matter.

It was at this time that Samuel was reacquainted with his family of origin. And it was at this point that he learned of his identity among the *Illumini*.

Ever since that day, it was a very rare occurrence that Luther would be unable to read the very essence of a person at first contact. That fact was what disturbed him now. He could *feel* his son inside of Marisha. He could *sense* his malevolent seed. But there was something else there too; he could not quite put his finger on it, but there was something present that he could not see.

But for the moment, Luther would not allow himself to become overly concerned. He knew that this boy would eventually be his greatest gift to his Master.

An honor, he thought, *my firstborn being so blessed.*

Luther beamed with malicious pride for a son not yet born, though this was only the beginning. He would have other sons, no doubt an entire legion of them.

iii

Dr. Sanger had temporarily stabilized Marisha's condition, but he emphasized to Jeffrey that any additional complications during delivery could prove very hazardous to both Marisha's and the twins' health. Either way, he expected to have to operate on Marisha after the delivery to prevent any further hemorrhaging.

The truth be known, Sanger was struggling with this entire process. It would be standard—most medically prudent—to deliver the twins by caesarean section due to the potentially ruptured uterus. Yet Luther had been clear; the children must be delivered vaginally. For the moment, Sanger was grateful that Jeffrey's knowledge of obstetrics was limited.

After making sure he was out of earshot of the fitfully sleeping Marisha, Jeffrey somewhat anxiously inquired, "Doc, can you tell by the ultrasound which baby will be delivered first?"

Sanger looked somewhat puzzled. He shrugged. "Well, one child definitely is in position to come out first, but I don't see what you mean as far as 'which' child?"

Jeffrey took a momentary glance in the opposite direction, then grabbed Dr. Sanger by the shirt and pushed him up against the wall. "What, I *mean*, big-boy, is which one is mine? Is it *my* child that is being born first?"

"Damn it, Jeffrey!" Dr. Sanger said, attempting to pull Jeffrey's hands off of him. "I have no way of knowing that! What difference does it—"

"It makes *all* the difference, Doctor," Jeffrey retorted, releasing the Sanger for the moment. "All the difference in the world! And let's be clear about this. I don't want anything to happen to my baby—he comes first. And I don't want anything to happen to Marisha either. As far as I'm concerned, the bastard twin can choke on his own cord. Do we understand each other, Doc?"

Sanger glared at him, and trying not to appear as one easily intimidated, he shot back, "You are sick, Jeffrey, you know that? I don't know why Luther keeps you around as Keeper of the Books, but I feel you should know this; my allegiance is to the Master, then Luther, and then my profession, and I will not make any exceptions for you! It's not my fault that you're not man enough to keep your woman under control."

At these last words, Jeffrey's eyes flared with rage as he clenched his hand into a fist, but he then thought better of it. He needed Sanger right now. But later, well, the good doctor might need a lesson in the concept of 'redemptive suffering'.

iv

"Holy Father, I must once more protest. This pilgrimage will be too dangerous. I beg you to reconsider."

But the Pontiff would not be dissuaded. "I have made a commitment, and I intend to keep it. I must go where the Spirit leads. I cannot let my decisions be dictated by fear."

The aide sighed. "Holy Father, you have taken many risks and placed yourself in a difficult position both within and outside of the Church—all for this alliance?"

"No, my good friend. All for Christ. Perhaps history will show this alliance to be an ill-fated one. Still, as my predecessor would like to say, '*Prophecy must be fulfilled.*' I must do what I do in good conscience and leave the rest to God. I serve at His pleasure."

"Must you hold your position so tenaciously, Holy Father? Will you not reconsider?"

With that, the earthly head of over a billion Catholics smiled gently. "Would you expect anything less from this tired old Olivetan?"

7

"The mind is its own place, and in itself can make a heaven of hell, and a hell of Heaven."

– John Milton

i

Jeffrey knelt by Marisha's side as she went into full labor, clutching her hand in his. Though the idea of any physical contact with Jeffrey usually repulsed her, she needed someone to be there for her. Her sister, Marisha had come to accept, had failed her. Maybe Vanya had built up a great deal of animosity towards her since her disappearance. The more she thought about it, she really couldn't blame Vanya for making her sleep in the bed she had made for herself.

"I can see a head," announced Dr. Sanger with a voice muffled through his surgical mask.

"Come on, baby," Jeffrey whispered. "This is it."

Marisha was panting heavily, sweat and tears trickling down both sides of her face. The pain was tremendous, yet bearable. She continued to find her mind wandering to the small bush she had planted on the grassy knoll. Locking onto the image gave her consolation and drew her into an affirming reality; she was soon to be a mother, and in spite of the circumstances, this was the moment she had been waiting for all her life.

"Keep pushing, Marisha," Dr. Sanger prodded.

She did. She had never wanted to push so hard, and with a tremendous groan too deep for words, half her battle was over. The first twin emerged, and Jeffrey gasped in joy.

"My son," he breathed in a barely audible whisper.

Dr. Sanger rubbed the baby's back fervently. The child gasped for air, then began to cry. Sanger cut the umbilical cord before handing the child to the nurse to attend to the various post-natal tasks. Sanger gave Jeffrey a nervous glance, then lowered his head to complete his charge.

Marisha, still panting, albeit slower, motioned to Jeffrey to lean closer so she could whisper to him. Jeffrey obliged her, noting the anomalous expression on her face, one that seemed as if she were a million miles away. It was a look that escaped him—that of serenity.

"Yes, Jeffrey," Marisha spoke in a weakened, yet resolute voice. "I too can feel that this is your son. But the other child, Jesse, will need a father also. You must promise me one thing, Jeffrey."

At this point, Jeffrey's sensation of self-absorbed euphoria overrode what he considered to be his own good judgment. "Anything, honey, anything."

"Promise that you will provide a mother figure for them also."

"A mother figure? Marisha what are you...?"

Instantly Marisha let out a reverberating wail. Dr. Sanger's eyes widened.

"What the—?"

Her entire body began to convulse. Her eyes rolled back into her head, and her mouth remained open, making sickening gargling sounds. Jeffrey began to back away in fear.

"What the hell's happening, Doc?" he whined. "Kill him, Doc! Don't let him do this to my—"

"Get him out of here!" Dr. Sanger commanded to two of his assistants.

Jeffrey lunged forward as they grabbed him. "Kill him, Doc! Kill him! Don't let him do this, don't let—"

The two men dragged Jeffrey kicking and screaming out into the hallway, calling out the name "Marisha" over and over again. Dr. Sanger stood there, frozen, trying to regain his composure.

It's only stress, he thought. *Get a hold of yourself, man, you're only seeing things!*

But no matter how many times Sanger repeated this mantra to himself, he could not get the image of what he had just seen out of his mind. He had thought he just about seen it all in delivering babies; caesarean sections, breech births, even severe deformities. But what he thought he saw emerge from Marisha's uterus, if only for an instant, would haunt his dreams for the duration of his life.

It was the mangled snout of a wild, snarling beast.

SEED

ii

Vanya was grateful when the flight ended. After circling for nearly an hour and a half due to some unknown complications, the plane was finally able to land. She headed straight for an airport phone and quickly dialed the number to Marisha's house. After three attempts, she still could not get an answer.

A feeling of desperation came over her.

Where could she be?

The answer came to her almost as quickly as she had asked it. Where else would a woman in her ninth month of pregnancy be?

The hospital!

Vanya quickly pulled out the phone book chained to the payphone and flipped through the pages. She did not know what hospital her sister would go to, but living in such a small town the options would probably be few.

On her second try, she hit pay dirt. Marisha had been admitted six hours ago. Vanya quickly checked out the car her uncle had secured for her, obtained some brief directions from the receptionist and headed for Ephesus Memorial Hospital.

It was pretty much a straight shot to the hospital, and Vanya expected about a thirty-five to forty-minute ride. A light drizzle started to fall as she began to ponder in what manner she would impose herself on the family. Marisha would be quick enough to be able to go along with whatever story Vanya initiated without raising even the slightest suspicion in anyone else. Her little sister was quite the pathological liar in her day, and Vanya never expected herself to be praying that Marisha had retained, if not refined, this quality.

The drizzle turned into a downpour of freezing rain, and Vanya was forced to slow her speed as her visibility dwindled to near zero. Thunder shook the ground she drove on. She quickly flipped on the radio, hoping to get a local news station. Turning on the scan mode, she watched as the numbers spiraled upwards, not locking on a single station.

All of a sudden, something small pelted the car. Then another, and still another. Vanya's eyes widened as, within an instant, the rental car was being completely bombarded by something.

A hailstorm? she thought.

She looked down at the digital readout on the radio. It read 120.1 and still rising.

>*That's odd*, she thought. *I could have sworn those things don't even go above 107 or 108.*

Vanya flipped the off switch, but to her surprise, it did not stop the scan. The display now read above 170 and seemed to be accelerating. Vanya began to notice that the temperature in the car, despite the cold December air, had increased to an uncomfortable level. However, she found the interior climate controls to be unresponsive. She felt the first trickle of sweat roll down the side of her cheek, but it was what happened next that sent a chill down her spine.

>*"Vanya."*

She jumped and attempted to slam on her brakes, but again the car's controls were unresponsive. It didn't seem to matter though. The objects were coming down so hard that Vanya could not see a thing. In fact, she did not even have the sensation of the car moving. There seemed to be a dull reddish glow illuminating from outside.

>"Who said that?" Vanya shrieked.

>*"Why have you forsaken me?"*

The voice was low-pitched, somewhat distant and distorted, but nonetheless familiar.

>"Marisha?" Vanya whispered apprehensively.

>*"You have left my children alone, unprotected!"*

Vanya finally looked down and saw that the radio had locked onto a channel. It read "616.0".

>"Oh, Marisha." Vanya was now beginning a frightened sob. "What has happened? I'm coming for you, please tell me what's—"

>*"You abandoned me when I needed you. For this, I cannot forgive you!"*

>"Please, Marisha," Vanya pleaded, feeling a sense of hysteria starting to overcome her. "Tell me where you are. I'm coming to get you!"

>*"Vanya."*

>"Yes, Marisha?"

>*"I AM IN HELL!"*

8

"The wailing of the newborn infant is intermingled
with the dirge for the dead."

– Lucretius

i

Dr. Sanger removed his surgeon's mask as he slumped down in his chair. He wiped the sweat from his forehead and tried to get his mind around what had just happened. It had been a long and trying delivery, but the second child had made it. Unfortunately, it was now his duty to tell Jeffrey that his spouse had not.

But what disturbed Sanger even more than the loss of his patient was the fact that he had hallucinated during the delivery. The second child was no more a wild beast than he was a Christian.

Years back, Mengel Sanger had been well known around campus in medical school for his homemade designer drugs and, admittedly, he had been his own best client. He had read documented cases in the medical journals of aftereffects taking place even decades after a person's drug use. He knew he would need to monitor himself.

Both children were now in the maternity ward, though the firstborn was much healthier and more responsive than the second. No matter now. Both were alive, though both would be deprived of the benefit of a mother, and with a father like Jeffrey, that was all the more devastating. A few hours old, and already behind in the struggle of life.

Dr. Sanger attempted to gather all the strength he could muster before he got up and walked out into the hallway. Jeffrey was sitting with his head in his hands out in the waiting area. When he saw Dr. Sanger, he jumped up from his seat and moved quickly towards him.

"Listen, Doc," Jeffrey began, anxiously. "I'm sorry about before...please tell me... is Marisha all right?"

"Why don't you come with me, Jeffrey, I'll show you your two sons first."

Jeffrey looked at him warily. "You mean my *one* son. The other's a bastard."

Dr. Sanger stifled his desire to respond to this comment. He brought Jeffrey up to the maternity ward and pointed out his son—the firstborn.

Jeffrey's eyes widened as he appeared to slip into another world. "Tobias," he whispered to himself.

"What was that?" Dr. Sanger questioned.

"What? Oh," Jeffrey said, snapping out of his trance. "I said Tobias. That's my boy's name. Tobias Isaac Chardin."

"And the other's name?" Dr. Sanger inquired.

"Where is he?" Jeffrey asked, his voice quickly transforming into a more aggravated tone.

"Just to the right of...uh...Tobias."

"Well, Marisha says she's naming him Jesse. To be honest with you, I don't give a shit. I'm not crazy about the idea of him carrying my last name either, but that's Luther's will, so I guess I'll have to live with it."

Jeffrey hesitated for a moment, obviously contemplating a thought which he found distasteful. However, his expression quickly changed.

"All right, terrific. I want to see Marisha now."

This was it. The good doctor looked up and down the hallway to see if any security guards were close by. No such luck.

"Ah... Jeffrey," he began, already seeing the expression on Jeffrey's face changing. "I'm sorry, I did everything I could, but Marisha didn't—"

And those were the last discernable words that would come from Dr. Sanger's mouth for the next six weeks. A right hook shattered his jaw in three places. Sanger was actually grateful when the follow-up punch knocked him unconscious. He really needed the rest.

SEED

ii

Sandy and Buzz Miller were driving down Interstate 55 after a less than sensational second honeymoon—a gift from their children for their 35th wedding anniversary. To top things off, the airline had lost their luggage on the return trip. However, the couple had managed to keep things on an even keel, and things were beginning to look up as they drove home from the airport.

It was a gorgeous, crisp day out with not a single cloud in the sky. Buzz had flipped on their favorite Golden Oldies station, and they were both harmonizing to the song *Wake up Little Suzie*.

They were about ten miles out from the airport when they spotted a car off to the side of the road halfway into Fred Peter's cornfield. Buzz decelerated, pulling up slowly to the side of the road. The sticker on the back identified the car as a rental. What the Millers saw next was quite odd, to say the least.

There was a woman with a fair complexion inside, and though the car was turned off, she was still pulling on the wheel as if she were steering. She seemed to be oblivious to the fact that her windshield wipers were speedily flapping and her headlights were on. But the strangest part of this picture was that the woman was screaming at someone or something as she kept trying to change the radio station.

Sandy and Buzz exchanged glances.

"Tourist," Buzz muttered.

They both burst into laughter as Buzz pulled the car back onto the road.

iii

Vanya stopped screaming when, in the blink of an eye, the entire scene transformed. She was now staring at a barren field and she realized she was gripping her rosary beads so hard that her knuckles were turning white.

"Please, Lord," she prayed, regaining her senses. "Let me not have been out of commission for as long as I was last time. Marisha needs me, and Lord knows, I need a therapist!"

Vanya pulled the car back onto the road, and resumed her journey into the unknown.

iv

Father Daniel Ananias knelt before the Blessed Sacrament gazing intently, yet lost in contemplation.

"You must intercede for her... and others to come... as will I."

He was still able to discern the voice of the Blessed Mother, the instrument God had chosen for the conversion of him and his family. Her voice had spoken to him as he gathered the consecrated hosts that had been spilled by an uncharacteristically hysterical Vanya Ciotola, one of Father Daniel's faithful daily communicants.

At the moment, in obedience, Father Daniel attempted to do just that, pray and intercede for this woman whom God clearly had a singular purpose for at this time. Yet the Spirit did not desire at the present moment to leave him there.

Father Daniel was perplexed as an image of his parents kept presenting itself in his mind's eye. It had been several decades since they had been killed—victims, along with many other Kurds, of the gassing of Saddam Hussein's regime. Had young Daniel not been on a coming-of-age hunting expedition with his uncle that day, he too would certainly have perished.

As he explored the image which drifted before him, his parents each placed their right hands on their hearts, bowed in a gesture of acknowledgement and respect, then stepped aside, dissolving from the image. Standing there behind his parents, Father Daniel recognized his paternal grandparents. Then they too stepped aside and faded, revealing more people behind them. This process continued, speeding up some, revealing a multitude of faces, some with a level of familiarity to them, others less so.

The images sped past and then stopped suddenly upon three men. They were dressed regally and could have passed for members of some ancient priestly caste, or even kings. With the same gesture, each bowed slightly in acknowledgement and then the process of faces passing resumed, finally resting on a single man.

His face was not only familiar, it was that of Daniel Ananias himself; different hair and clothes but the resemblance was unmistakable.

The apparent self-image was reclined, lying across the belly of a great lion, which looked up and met eyes with Father Daniel. As the vision continued, the self-image looked at Father Daniel with a steady gaze while maintaining a

SEED

gentle smile. He lifted a chalice, upon which were inscribed seven names:

Vanya   Paula   Annie   Nathaniel   Siro   Phineas   Felipe

"Do not let this cup pass, Daniel... taste its bitterness... drink of its suffering..."

Father Daniel hesitated. Had he not suffered enough already? Had he not given all for the sake of the Cross?

"Countless souls rest in the balance, Daniel. Trust that the God who has led you here will not abandon you. The time of His Mercy is coming to a close. His justice cannot be held back any longer. The cup is about to overflow."

Father Daniel felt a wave of fear grip him. Could he handle much more? He felt he had "arrived" upon being made Rector of the Cathedral Basilica of Saints Peter and Paul. He had done his time, and the Lord had rewarded him. Now He asked for more?

"For this, you were born. For this, you have been called..."

Daniel suddenly felt a comforting, maternal presence about him, and all fear and hesitation ceased. He reached out, took the cup, and drank deeply of it. It was indeed bitter, and it made his very innards burn to the point of swooning. Yet there was also something else in the mystical drink, was it Truth? Was it... Love?

Father Daniel lost focus, and the vision faded.

"Your will, Lord, not mine," he whispered as he blessed himself, wiping the moisture from his eyes (no doubt invoked by the vivid image of his beloved parents) before exiting the chapel.

9

"...the fog is rising."

– Emily Dickinson's last words

i

Jeffrey stood over the gravesite as Luther spoke. A light snow had begun, soon to blanket the entire frozen ground. A dark set of sunglasses masked his bloodshot eyes. He was still feeling numb, and he knew he would be for sometime. He felt a deep... *absence*, but even more so, he was angry. Angry at Marisha for having an affair. Angry at Jesse, the bastard twin, for killing his spouse. Angry because he could not figure out what was next.

What the hell am I going to do with two kids and no wife?

Jeffrey had raised this question with Luther, who assured him that the Master would provide. Luther claimed to have foreseen the coming of a woman, faithful to the Master, who would serve in the role of both nanny and teacher to the twins. Jeffrey would have to wait and trust.

Up above the gravesite, partly hidden by a large oak tree, Vanya knelt on the ground praying a Divine Mercy Chaplet, yearning with all her heart, strength, and soul that her sister would throw herself at the mercy of her God. Tears streamed down Vanya's cheeks, but she felt a renewed strength permeating her body and spirit with each word.

She had been too late, and Marisha had died believing her sister, and most likely her God, had abandoned her. As distraught as Vanya felt, she knew she would have to garner all of her strength to follow through with the task at hand. Without her sister's help, Vanya would have to figure out how to protect the children on her own, and she did not have a clue as to how to accomplish this.

Oh Blood and water which gushed forth from the Heart of Jesus, as a fountain of mercy for us, I trust in You.

As Vanya finished up her final prayer, an extraordinary sight caught her eye up on the grassy knoll above the ceremony. There, just behind a seemingly out-of-place shrub-like plant stood the well-dressed man from her vision. As she got up to move towards him, the funeral congregation began to dissipate. The well-dressed man turned his back and began to walk away.

Vanya quickened her pace as the man was almost out of sight, heading down the other side of the hill. She finally arrived at the spot where he had been standing to find no trace of him. The grass was higher where she stood but showed no sign of having been trampled.

Get a grip, Vanya, she thought. *Now is not the time to start losing it!*

She began to walk away, feeling disappointed, but then she hesitated.

Wait a minute...did he say *something to me?*

Vanya stood in place, thoroughly perplexed. Something was echoing in her short-term memory that had not been there before.

No, that's not it. He didn't say anything. Maybe... maybe he thought *something to me.*

Vanya knelt again, clearing her mind. What came back to her was so simple, yet in her mind, certain suicide.

Go to him.

There was no doubt about it, and she knew, just *knew*, that he meant Jeffrey. Just show up without a plan? That was crazy, she was sure of that. But for some reason, the more she thought of it the more acceptable the notion became to her. She had reached this point in her life on faith, and she was not about to abandon it now.

Looking down from where she stood, Vanya saw that the entire funeral procession had now departed, apparently walking to a nearby house for some form of reception. She looked both ways, then guardedly walked to the gravesite. Upon reaching the casket, already having been lowered into the carefully carved-out ditch, she pulled a flask from her coat.

"Forgive Marisha, Lord, for all of her shortcomings. In her own way, I believe she came back to You in these past months. Please heal her tormented soul and accept her into Your Kingdom. Amen."

Vanya opened the flask and spread holy water over the casket in the sign of the cross. She then pulled the rosary from her pocket, kissed it, and released it into the grave.

"Goodbye, Marisha."

And with that, Vanya broke down. The pain which she had never allowed herself to feel, even upon her husband's death, came roaring forth in a flood of tears. Vanya looked up to the sky, begging for the peace that eluded her. Still, she felt a resolve in her. She would move forward.

Let it be done to me, according to Thy will.

ii

Vanessa Ami-Richards, a tough-looking young beauty in her prime, had her bags packed and was now on a train heading east. She did not know who she was meeting. She did not know where she was going. All she knew was that she had had a vision the night before, and a messenger from the Master had instructed her to get on this train. As a thirteen-year veteran of the Temple of Shaat, she was not about to disobey her charge.

Vanessa's train car was nearly empty, only a handful of others were riding with her, for a handful of different reasons. An uptight-looking businessman tapped incessantly on the keyboard of his laptop. A young lady who looked like a model was accompanied by her son, who enthusiastically pointed out the window at different objects that caught his interest. There was young couple dressed mostly in formal black, their eyes bloodshot, with a baby girl not more than five or six months old clutched in the mother's arms. And finally, there was a disgusting looking man in the corner who must have been some kind of transient. Had she noticed this man when she boarded, Vanessa probably would have chosen another car. But she had already selected a seat, and besides, the bum was sleeping. How much harm could he cause?

She turned her left arm upward, revealing a tattoo of a serpent biting a woman's heel. When anxious, she always looked to this mark to comfort herself. It reminded her of the wonderful life-changing decision she had made so many years ago; a decision that moved her out of her past victimhood and into roles of domination and power.

So focused was she on her reminiscing with the tattoo that Vanessa didn't even notice the eyes of the shabbily dressed man open and fix upon her.

Her eyes suddenly were opened to a single, terrifying glimpse of eternity as the state of her soul was made manifest.

SEED

iii

Luther arrived back at his Temple incensed. In his internal battle between logic and rage, rage definitely had the upper hand at the moment. He knocked over the coat rack, and then sent dozens of glasses and plates sprawling. They crashed to the ground, echoing through the corridors, then leaving an eerie silence.

"Why can't I see? Why can't I SEE?" he raged.

It was obvious that he was not referring to his eyes. Luther was able to find every item he wished to decimate without a problem. A lamp served as a good target for him to kick. It sailed across the room, then upon reaching its cord's full extension, pulled back and smashed on the ground.

He stared out intently into nothingness. "Master, why have you not granted me full dominion yet? If I cannot see *all*, how may I subdue your subjects?"

No answer came, but in truth, Luther did not need one. He knew that he would not begin the final phase of his spiritual growth until the boy fulfilled the role for which he was born. That would be nearly seven years from now.

He grabbed at the sides of his head, preparing for the unavoidable migraine, then paused momentarily, struck by an idea. He moved over towards the cabinet at the far side of the room. With a renewed effort of constraint, Luther opened it and pulled out a piece of rubber tubing, wrapping it around his upper arm. He was panting heavily yet steadily as he drew out the syringe.

"Just a little pinprick," he moaned as he cleared the needle head of air.

He plunged the needle into his vein, releasing the venom ever so slowly. When he had released all the fluid from the syringe, Luther pulled out the needle and released the rubber tubing. A sigh of relief and exhilaration escaped from his lips.

It had been a roller coaster of a week. His son had been born, though the mother had died at birth.

*I had so much wanted to see her eyes when I offered her...*our....*son, to the Master,* he mused.

He had fantasized about future encounters with this woman—especially following the forced exile of his secretary-harlot, the not-too-swift Delilah Hagarot. Yet he had not foreseen Marisha's death.

Nor did Luther know what to think about the burial ceremony. He had felt a presence at one part of the ritual—an unwelcome presence. It was only for an instant, and Luther did not believe that any of his followers had noticed the minuscule change in the pitch of his voice. They might have interpreted this as a sign of weakness, or even compassion, which he of course could not, *would* not, allow.

Still, there was much work to be done, and much preparation over the next few years. He had to be content with the knowledge that the Master would send a woman to train the boy. He was intrigued to see what she would be like, as he had barely been able to envision her.

What was her name? Something like Van, or Vanna.

Anyway, at the moment its importance was fading. He was done thinking, done worrying. Dr. Sanger's designer drug was beginning to take effect. Luther climbed onto the couch, leaned back into a comfortable position and prepared himself for an enjoyable trip.

iv

"Hey, Felix, come quickly! You are not going to believe this!"

Felix Amosov moved hurriedly into the room, where he found his boss looking at the television.

"It is all over the news. The Pope has been assassinated on his pilgrimage to Iraq!"

Amosov's eyes widened. "You cannot be serious, Alex. Who would want to kill the Pope? Nobody takes him seriously anymore."

Nesterov looked sternly at his friend and subordinate. "Think, man!"

Amosov stared curiously at Nesterov. "Surely you do not believe our supreme leader of the motherland is behind this?"

"And why would I not believe it?"

Amosov looked incredulously at the television as he popped another stick of nicotine gum into his mouth. "Look, Alex, you see there, it was an Islamic Fundamentalist that killed him. This is nothing more than the result of that ill-begotten alliance he made with those insane Muslims. I know many liked the sound of it, but it was extremely naïve. Now this is what his own foolishness has gotten him. Hardliners on both sides hated him for it."

"What you say may very well be true, Felix, but your assessment is even more naïve. For decades, our *esteemed* leader of Mother Russia," Nesterov's sarcasm was obvious here, "made his own alliances with these same Muslim leaders—so much so, to the outside observer, you would think he was Muslim himself."

"I had my suspicions! Always with an angle—as a good Russian should!" Amosov grinned as he glanced at the television, which now displayed anti-Papal celebrations and demonstrations across the Islamic world.

"But truth be told," Nesterov continued, "they were nothing but pawns in his hands. He was successful in inciting these ideologues to fight Western democratic and capitalistic power everywhere in the world. And with what result?"

Amosov shrugged. "The Americans did not have the... what do our Italian friends say? The *cajones* to finish out the war in Iraq or Afghanistan. The country was divided, they pulled out in shame, and then..."

"...and then the single superpower left in the world began its slow leak of worldwide influence. America, she still leaks today. So who then, but Mother Russia, to take her place?"

Amosov looked intrigued, but still not fully convinced. "So then what is our supreme leader's intention? Even if he is using the Islamic world as pawns for his own agenda, all he has succeeded in doing is empowering and spreading the Islamic faith. He has made his own miscalculation just like the Pope... ahhh... forgive me, ex-Pope."

Nesterov shook his head. "You must recognize, Felix. In his mind, the Soviet Union never ended, it only went underground for a period of time, and some of our former colleagues even hinted that this was completely, and brilliantly, I might add, orchestrated to lull the West into a false sense of security."

"But what of the Muslims?"

"Remember, Felix, the leader of the motherland is a true believer, a Communist in every molecule of his being. His assessment of Islam is that it will implode from within. This assassination is perfect. I have to give the *huesos* his due. World opinion—the most fickle of all opinions known—will now come down against the Muslims."

"But most of the world hated this Pope, Alex! Most considered him a throwback and wanted to send him back to ancient Gaul, where he came from!"

Nesterov just stared for a moment at his subordinate. "Felix, it is good that you came with me to serve in this 'business' because your political naïveté is unprecedented. It does not matter what the world *thought* of this poor Pope. Our *good* leader, may he *kooshi govne ee oomree*, will use every resource at his disposal to make this poor Pope out to be the would-be savior of our modern times. All anonymously, of course. He himself will only have a few nice words to say."

"And then what?"

"Then the world turns on Islam, Islam begins its own infighting, and in the process, the new and reconstituted Soviet Union returns."

Amosov shook his head and chuckled. "Brilliant, Alex, somewhat farfetched perhaps, but brilliant nonetheless. Tell me, why did you ever leave the motherland? It seems like you would have had a great future in the political scene there."

Nesterov cocked a skeptical eyebrow. "A great future, or an early grave? No Felix, I am apolitical. My allegiance is not to an idea but to my family. The power I seek is not through politics, but through strength. Once I have my family back and in order, I will institute many changes in our 'family business'. Within three years, our operations will be completely legitimate and above board. We will be good and honest citizens of this once great country."

Amosov looked surprised. "And what will Ivankov think of this?"

Nesterov hesitated only for a moment, then spoke barely above a whisper. "It was actually his idea, Felix. He has grown rich in wealth and weary in bloodshed. We have the American dream with a Russian heart, Felix. There is no need to continue down this path."

Amosov stared carefully at his boss, momentarily ceasing his incessant gum chewing. "I cannot believe this will happen. I know you. I know Ivankov. You cannot leave this once you are in."

Nesterov glanced briefly at the door, still ajar, leading to the next room, where several of his men were casually speaking. He beckoned to Amosov to lean closer, then whispered solemnly.

"There is trouble down the pike, which I do not believe Vlad will be able to overcome even with all of our help. Sides will be taken, Felix. For me, I wish to be on neither. I will do all in my power to protect my family in this, and then I want out. You would be wise to do the same, my friend. When you are approached to be a 'voice of reason' to me, a 'mediator between factions', if you will, it is then that you will know this *sooka* as my betrayer. For I will lead no faction, I will claim no dominion save that which has been given me in blood."

10

i

Jeffrey sat on the sofa with his head between his hands. Luther had moved him to a new dwelling in a more populated area about a half-mile from the Temple. Here, Jeffrey would not be far from his children when he carried out his tasks for the Coven. Yet at the moment, this close proximity was not a pleasant thought for Jeffrey to mull over.

The twins had been brought home about an hour ago, and they were crying uncontrollably. By this time, Jeffrey was grinding his teeth, trying to pull himself together.

I'm going to lose it!

He had to do something. He had lost his wife, he didn't know the first thing about childcare, and he was almost finished with his last bottle of Bacardi Rum without even so much as a buzz.

He grabbed the remote control and flipped the television on, raising the volume to a near deafening level in attempts to block out the twin's crying. He flipped through the channels. A reality show. A soap opera. A train crash in Smyrna.

Smyrna, that's only an hour from here.

Jeffrey watched briefly but was disappointed to find that only one passenger had died, and strangely enough, that was of an apparent heart attack. Evidently, the investigators were stumped as to the identity of the elderly woman, as she carried the identification of a thirty-three-year-old female. Her only identifying mark was a tattoo on the inside of her forearm of a snake biting a woman's heel. This was just the ticket to ease the tension. Jeffrey chuckled to himself. "Grandma pickpocket!"

The doorbell rang and Jeffrey jumped. He scrambled for his remote control and shut the television off. The twins were still screaming. He glanced in their direction as he moved towards the door. Why was his heart beating so hard? It even seemed as if the hair on the back of his neck was standing on end. He moved anxiously towards the door, reaching for the doorknob, and as he opened the door, the twins stopped crying.

There, standing in his doorway, was a beautiful young lady, perhaps in her mid-twenties. Jeffrey had to blink because for a split second he thought it was Marisha.

"Good day, Mr. Chardin, my name is Vanya and I—"

Jeffrey moved aside to clear the doorway. "Yes, yes, thank the devil you're here. I've been expecting you."

Vanya stopped dead in mid-sentence. She tried, unsuccessfully, to hide her astonishment. Was this a trap?

"Expecting me? Sir, I—"

"Well, yes, of course," Jeffrey responded. "You are the woman Luther told me about, aren't you? You know, to take care of the kids."

Vanya regained her composure, quickly masking her surprise. "Well, yes, Mr. Chardin, I am. But you will have to forgive me. I was not filled in on many of the details."

"Well isn't that the way things always are?" Jeffrey remarked in an uncharacteristically charitable fashion, his visible relief overriding his generally poor demeanor. "Anyway, why don't I start by showing you the twins? Your primary responsibility will be to keep them quiet and out of my hair."

"Of course, sir," Vanya responded, already sizing Jeffrey up, wondering what her sister could possibly have seen in this man.

They walked back to the spare bedroom, where they found the two boys lying on a bed. They obviously needed changing, and most likely food as well. Vanya couldn't help but wonder if Jeffrey would have let these children starve out of his own ignorance.

"They're precious!" she remarked, realizing she had just set eyes on her two nephews.

"Well, you're half right," Jeffrey responded absently. "This one here is my son, Tobias Isaac. This other one's a bastard. My wife, rest her soul, did not hold the seal of marriage as sacred as I did."

Vanya moved closer, making eye contact with the twin Jeffrey had so lovingly identified as a "bastard."

"And what is your name, little one?"

Jeffrey responded, his irritation still evident. "His name's Jesse. Marisha named him before... before he killed her. I would just as soon have left him there at the hospital, but Luther has plans for that one. I guess I'm stuck."

Vanya had not heard a single word past the phrase 'his name is Jesse'. She stood there, staring, dumbfounded by what was happening. Could it be coincidence that this boy had the same name as the shepherd boy in her vision? She thought not. Though it should not surprise her when the hand of her Lord acted in such a clear and obvious manner, it was still comforting to know she was not on her own.

What, Lord, are you orchestrating here? What are you asking of me?

But there was only silence. Vanya would have to be satisfied that her God would reveal what He needed her to know in time. The words that came from the lips of the shepherd boy were still ringing in her ears. And what had he said? She had been "chosen"?

"Vanya! HELLO! Earth to Vanya!"

It was Jeffrey's voice. She had let herself slip.

"Yes... ah... Mr. Chardin?"

"Are you all right, Vanya? Your face turned white and your entire expression changed. It looked like you zoned out on me."

"Oh dear," she responded. "I'm sorry, it's just that—"

"No matter," Jeffrey interrupted. "The little bastard has that same effect on me too. Kind of creepy, isn't he?"

"Sir?"

"Creepy but... I'll be damned. He sure seems taken by you."

Vanya looked down again to see little Jesse smiling up at her. She looked back uncomfortably at Jeffrey, trying to feign a smile. Jeffrey moved towards the door.

"Anyway, Vanya, I have got to get ready for work. I'll leave money for you on the kitchen table to get groceries and whatever else they might need. We'll go over your responsibilities tonight when I get back. And when you take them out, stay within a mile's proximity of the house. Trust me on this one."

"Yes, Mr. Chardin."

Jeffrey got himself ready and was out the door within an hour. Vanya wondered if it was normal for him to go off to work with alcohol on his breath. No matter. She had already bathed, changed, and fed the babies some formula that the hospital had provided. She went back into the room where they lay, the two seemingly fascinated with one another.

"Well, boys, it looks like I'm in it for the long haul."

She began stroking their torsos, which they both seemed to enjoy. Though the logical course of action would seem to be to take the children and run as fast as she could, she somehow sensed this would not be possible—it was not the path she had been called to take.

The parable about the wheat and the weeds had been running through her head all day. The farmer was not to pull the weeds until they and the wheat had grown to the point where they could be distinguished. So too must she wait for the right time with these children.

Vanya pulled the flask from her coat and leaned over Tobias. She began pouring holy water over his head.

"Tobias Isaac, I baptize you in the name of the Father, the Son..."

ii

Alexandre Nesterov paced back and forth in his office. Felix Amosov, along with another one of his men, stood by, anxiously awaiting their superior's commands. When Nesterov, a man normally fairly cool under pressure, was this fired-up, somebody ended up getting hurt. Worse, somebody usually ended up getting killed. Once again he had been blindsided. And once again, it was by his own progeny.

"*Chyort viz'mi!* What does she think she's doing?" he ranted.

Nesterov picked up the telegram lying on his desk for the tenth time, making sure he had not missed something the first nine times through.

Papa-

Went to get Marisha. No time to explain. Will be in contact soon.

With love, Vanya

He slammed his fist down on his desk. "*Chto za huy!* I expected this kind of behavior from Marisha, but Vanya? This is unthinkable!"

Nesterov sat down in his chair, placed his hands on his desk and took a deep breath. Not a moment later, his demeanor had completely transformed. It was amazing how quickly this man could regain his composure.

"Gavrilenkov!" he boomed.

The gentleman on the left stepped forward.

"Yes, Mr. Nesterov." His response was reminiscent of a newly initiated cadet responding to his drill sergeant.

Nesterov had, at this point, assessed the situation in his mind and was ready for action. "It sounds like Vanya left in some hurry, which means she was probably not very careful in covering her tracks. She should not be hard to find. When you discover her location, do nothing until you report back to me. Do you understand?"

"Yes, Mr. Nesterov." These were pretty much the only three words Andrey Gavrilenkov ever spoke to his boss, which was fine with him. As he had been told time and time again, he was not paid to think, much less debate. He swiftly exited the room.

Amosov shadowed Gavrilenkov for a moment before closing the double doors behind him. He returned to Nesterov and sat down in the chair next to him.

"What's going on, Alex?" he inquired.

"What is going on?" Alexandre Nesterov repeated, leaning forward on his desk. There was a hint of uncharacteristic despair in his voice as he asked the same question himself.

It continued to be uncomfortable for Amosov to see this side, this *weaker* side, of his boss and friend. Though he was only four years younger, Amosov had found a father figure in Nesterov when he, barely a teenager, was called upon to serve under him briefly in the Russian-Afghani war. The years following in his footsteps (and somewhat in his shadow), through the GRU, the clandestine years in Israel, and finally in his emigration to the United States, were some of the best years of discipleship anyone could have hoped for.

Nesterov's countenance quickly degraded into one of disgust. "This entire world, it is going to hell in a handbasket! What is happening, you ask? I do not know! That is the truth! Everything is spinning out of control! I have not known the whereabouts of my own daughter for a year now! This is not acceptable! Do you hear what I am saying?"

Amosov nodded. "I hear you, Alex. I too am at a loss."

Nesterov leaned back and let out a sigh. "I cannot afford to be at a loss, Felix. I sense the breaking down within the syndicate as well, and with that, I could lose many resources at my disposal to draw my family back together. Yerik has had no success in finding Marisha. So now I do this, Caputo's concern about using syndicate resources for personal matters be damned!"

"I am with you, Alex. All the way."

Nesterov's expression grew solemn as he looked over to Amosov. "Still, I do not know, Felix. I did my share of checking up on this Chardin character. I cannot rush into this one shooting, even if I do discover his whereabouts."

"Yes, I remember us checking him out."

That was an understatement. They now knew just about everything there was to know about Jeffrey Chardin, from when he was toilet trained all the way to how he cheated on the bar exam. It had taken months just to confirm his last name. But now they had all the info on him anyone could ask. All, that is, except for his location.

"Well, his supposed involvement with the occult spooks me." Nesterov looked over to Amosov, knowing the expression he would have on his face. Amosov did not disappoint. Nesterov continued. "Yes, you heard me right. I did not want the good Bishop Kashira, or more importantly, Vlad Ivankov, learning that my daughter had hooked up with some Satan-freak, so I kept that under my hat."

"*S'ebis'!* Alex, what would Marisha be doing—?"

"Do you not think that I have asked myself that question?" Nesterov retorted. "Do you not think that I wonder each night what kind of God-forsaken group she has gotten herself in with? The best I can do is believe she was kept ignorant on the matter. Marisha is many things, but she is no worshiper of the devil!"

"Of course not, Alex. Not Marisha."

Though Amosov's curiosity had been piqued, he knew not to pursue this area of the discussion any further. "What can I do?"

"Right now, we wait. I am not sure if Vanya knows fully what she is getting into. But she has a very sharp head on her shoulders; she is her father's daughter after all. Once we locate her and assess the situation, we will then decide how to make contact with her. I am afraid that I have no choice at this time but to trust her judgment."

"Just give me the word, Alex, and I will nail this *ebanatyi pidaraz* to a cross!"

Nesterov chuckled. Amosov's friendship and loyalty did not go unnoticed by him. He was the last of his men to have been at his side since their youth. As Nesterov pondered Amosov's comment for a moment, his grin transformed into something with a more sinister flair.

"I do not plan to let him off that easy."

11

Allied Press   ~

GENEVA - Following three weeks of
ongoing negotiations with the U.N.
Security Council, the Ugandan delegation
has pulled out of the talks stating:
"The United Nations, the supposed
brokers of peace, are blinded by their
own ideology to the true origin of these
conflicts."

The fighting on the African
continent of both anti- and pro-
government militias has entered its
third month, and is now encompassing
seven countries. Karl Weishaupt, the
Secretary General of the United Nations,
was quoted as saying: "The African
Conflict is quickly expanding to the
degree where U.N. intervention on a
military level will no longer be a
viable option."

Weishaupt has delayed military
action by the U.N. to this point,
believing that a political solution
could be found to the conflict. "It has
become impossible to tell where
divisions have been drawn; it is true,
some are still along tribal and ethnic
lines, but more and more are clearly
demarked by religious affiliation. We
see clearly once again the dangers of
any religion which makes non-inclusive
claims on the truth."

Though there are no indications of
the use of nuclear or chemical weapons
at this time, it is suspected that at
least four of the estimated twelve
warring factions may possess some form
of nuclear device. Over 300 such devices
still remain unaccounted for after the
fall of the Soviet Union.

Most political experts agree that the prospect of a rapid decline in demand for oil due to the imminent production of newer and safer alternative fuels, as well as the recent assassination of the Catholic Pope, have served as catalysts which have allowed old unresolved internal conflicts to surface.

i

The first two weeks had gone by as smoothly as Vanya could have hoped. She knew that her "free" time was limited; this was the day she had instructed her friend to forward a telegram to her father. It had been her intent to fully assess the situation by the time her father found her, yet she had to admit; there was some security in knowing that if something went wrong, with her current tracks not hidden very well, her father would find her.

The reality of the situation was grim, but not hopeless. Jeffrey was rarely home, so Vanya could pretty much do as she pleased with the children. It was actually his suggestion, ironically, that they refer to her as "Nanny Vanya." She knew she had to be careful though. Jeffrey treated Tobias like a prince, buying him toys and playing with him frequently. She had a difficult time accepting this softer side of Jeffrey. It was a paradox for her; the man whom she ultimately held responsible for the death of her beloved sister now lived under the same roof as she, showing such compassion, albeit superficial, to the motherless Tobias.

Jesse was a different story, and it was here that the true colors of this monster showed forth. Jeffrey would taunt, poke, and prod at Jesse. It was also not uncommon for Jeffrey to spit on him on the not-infrequent occasions when he came home drunk or high. Vanya cried every time she found a new bruise on the boy, offering up her desperate prayers to a God who seemed strangely silent. She had to choose her battles wisely with Jeffrey though; if she pushed too hard, she risked the possibility of her expulsion, leaving the children with no protection at all.

Tonight would be Vanya's most dangerous obstacle thus far. Luther was returning from a trip out east, and he wished to have dinner at their home. More importantly, Luther wished to meet the twins and their new nanny. Vanya had just finished setting the table when she heard the front door open.

"Vanya?" It was Jeffrey's voice.

She moved quickly into the foyer to meet them. On her way she prayed a quick 'Hail Mary' and made the sign of the cross. As she walked around the corner and first set eyes on Luther, a chill shot through her body. He met her gaze and smiled.

"Why, good day, Miss...?"

"Davino, but please, sir, call me Vanya."

"Very well," Luther responded. "Vanya it is."

Something did not feel quite right to Vanya. She felt naked standing in front of this man, as if thousands of probing eyes were scanning her both inside and out.

Be gone, Satan, she prayed.

Luther blinked. Or was it more of a flinch? Either way, it was only for an instant, and he regained his composure quickly, a conceited grin returning to his face.

"Uh, Vanya?" It was Jeffrey speaking. "Aren't you going to offer to take Father's coat?"

"Oh, forgive me, I was just, well, taken by such a striking gentleman that you have brought to dinner. Please, sir, let me get that for you."

Her comment made Luther raise an eyebrow. He was not so mature that he was immune to flattery. He smiled affectionately at Vanya, having seemingly forgotten whatever it was that had irritated him a moment earlier.

"Well, shall we see the boys?" Jeffrey offered.

"By all means," Luther responded, nodding to Vanya.

As Jeffrey led Luther away into the twin's room, Vanya breathed a sigh of relief. While she believed that the nature of each man was created good, though wounded, her experience of Luther was that of a perfectly corrupted soul. Vanya also picked up on the fact that he had a sort of sixth sense of his own. She would have to keep her guard up at all times with him. She walked back into the kitchen and began mixing drinks for the men.

Luther was taken at the sight of the boys. Though Jeffrey had intended to first lead him to his own son, Tobias, Luther immediately moved towards Jesse.

"Ah, Father, that's the bastard, this is—"

Luther turned towards Jeffrey with a fiery stare. "What did you call him?"

Jeffrey turned white. He had forgotten himself. "I'm sorry, Father, I just—"

Moving quickly into a feigned presentation of control, Luther interjected, "*You are less than nothing, and as nothing, you shall be silent!*" he seethed. "This child is the future of our kind. The plan for this one will be our catalyst into the world to come! You must never forget the importance of his life!"

"Yes, Father." Jeffrey choked on his own words, being thoroughly shamed. No, he did not have to like Jesse, or necessarily even treat him well. But he did have to make sure he lived to fulfill his destiny.

Whatever that is! And may I not be there to see it!

"It is your calling to serve as foster father to this child up to the appointed time of his... *liberation*. You must also see to it that that woman teaches both him and your child our ways."

Luther paused, apparently sinking into a deep thought. As he turned towards the open door, a look of concern came over his face. "What do you know about her, Jeffrey?" he asked.

"Who, Vanya?" Jeffrey was glad to jump topics as quickly as possible. He shrugged. "Well, not too much. She showed up as you told me she would. She's excellent with the children, and she comes highly recommended."

"Recommended?" Luther lifted an eyebrow.

"Yes, I just received her references a week ago. Elder Counselor Aquar, of the Temple of Shaat, as well as Senator William Maison, gave her a glowing report. They both report her as a loyal servant to the Faith and tremendous with the development of the youth. I really couldn't be more pleased with what she has done here."

"Hmmmm," Luther was again contemplating.

"Is something troubling you, Father?" Jeffrey inquired.

Luther was not about to admit to Jeffrey that he could not see into Vanya's soul. He felt nothing from her except a thick wall. However, he was very aware that members of the Temple of Shaat were known for their discipline in mind control.

"No, nothing is wrong," Luther answered. "Just... just *monitor* her. She is new to our people. I do not want her to be informed of our plan for the child yet. Is that clear, Jeffrey?"

"Crystal, Father. Shall we eat?"

Luther grinned. "Yes, my son. And will Vanya be joining us?"

Jeffrey looked a bit perplexed. "Why, I had not planned on it, Father. She usually eats in the kitchen while she feeds the children."

"I would request her company at the dinner table."

Jeffrey shrugged. "Very well, Father. I'm sure she'd be honored."

Luther left that night with two servings of lamb in his belly, along with a large portion of frustration.

Why can I not read her?

He had attempted to pick up on Vanya for the entire meal, but to no avail. He felt her blocking him, resisting him. He had experienced difficulty reading others in the past, and only occasionally did what he could not see cause a problem for him. Still, the idea of not being able to read someone so close to him was unsettling to say the least.

I must have faith in the Master's decision.

Yes, that was about all he could do at this time. He would have Jeffrey keep an extra close eye on Vanya, and he would monitor his son's progress himself, away from Vanya. This plan would prevent any damage which she could possibly do, while also allowing him to avoid the displeasure of spending time with someone who was so... *disconcerting.*

Vanya calmly yet quickly moved herself to the bathroom. She vomited three times with barely enough time to gasp for breath between each upheaval. Her head was throbbing. Who was this man? And how could he have such a horrible effect on her?

Once she had lost about everything she had to lose, she sat back against the bathroom wall. Sweat poured down her face, and a chill traversed her body. She was shivering, and she now realized that her nose was bleeding.

"You all right?" It was Jeffrey calling out from downstairs, her knight in shining armor.

"Fine, Mr. Chardin, thank you. Just a little headache that's all."

"Well then, get your ass down here and fix me a drink!"

I can see why my sister fell so in love with him!

Vanya got up and splashed water on her face. She could feel her strength slowly returning. Though Luther had tried all evening to pick up something on her, she was fairly certain that she had not given him anything to work with. It had required a concerted effort throughout the meal, but she hoped that his frustration would cause him to give up on her instead of envisioning her as a challenge.

She had passed her most difficult task to date. The next task, however, would be twice as difficult. She would have to convince her father to do nothing for the time being.

ii

The now-former Konstantin Cardinal Christov sat in a small room within the walls of the Sistine Chapel. At the ripe old of age of thirty-nine, the youthful Primate of the Catholic Church in Russia had just emerged from the Papal Conclave elevated to the highest office in Christianity.

I have done it. For this I was born!

The room Konstantin sat in had, over the years, been dubbed "the crying room," the place where the full realization of the office would finally overwhelm the Pope-Elect, resulting in tears of humble gratitude. However, at this moment there were no tears falling from Konstantin's eyes. The feeling that moved within him could better be described as exhilaration.

He gazed with pride at the pallium that hung before him. He would wear this as, not much more than an hour from now, he would stun billions announcing a "New Reformation", forming the Church in *his own* image, throwing off the manmade shackles of history which had prevented the Church from engaging the world in a more realistic, more contemporary, and less holier-than-thou fashion.

"Christopher."

SEED

Konstantin was startled by a voice which emerged from behind him, and he quickly wheeled around to see two men standing before him. The first, well-dressed and stately; the second, like a vagabond off the streets.

"Who are you?" Konstantin exclaimed indignantly. "What is the meaning of this?"

"Do not be afraid, Christopher," the vagabond spoke.

"I am certainly not afraid," Konstantin retorted, reminding himself of his own regality. He was about to speak again, but then hesitated as a curious recognition passed through his consciousness. "You speak to me in the Russian mother tongue, though the dialect which you use has not been spoken for at least a century."

"You would prefer something more... *contemporary*, Christopher?" the vagabond continued.

"That will not be necessary. I am a linguist and speak more than three dozen languages and dialects fluently."

"We know this, Christopher." Again the vagabond spoke, with the stately dressed man remaining curiously silent.

Konstantin generated a look of disgust on his face, turning his stare towards the silent man. "What is this? You have a rogue serving as your mouthpiece? Do you two share a brain?" Then, looking back at the other, "And why must you insist on referring to me by a Latinized form of my surname?"

"Does it make a difference from what mouth the truth is spoken?"

"Truth? What is truth but that which those who are in power say it is?"

"Christopher," the vagabond continued, "is your name, given not by man, but *Elohim* above."

"Well then it will disappoint you greatly," Konstantin asserted, "to know that I have already informed the cardinals that I am to take the name Peter II. I shall bring the Church full circle."

"*That* name has not been given to you; it is for another to come."

Konstantin stared at the two unlikely companions that stood before him, not liking the disadvantage he felt at this moment. He grappled in his mind to gather his thoughts, to make some sense of this strange situation. A light seemed to emerge from his muddled head.

"I believe I am beginning to understand," he began. "You two have been sent by those fascist traditionalists, possibly charged by my predecessor, to intimidate me to keep the Church in the dark ages."

The two exchanged curious, if not amused, glances.

"The Church is in need of conversion!" Konstantin contended.

"It is you who are in need of conversion, Christopher."

"I do not believe you understand what the reality of the situation is here!" Konstantin struggled to maintain his regal air yet digressed into frustrated argument. "I have been prepared for this office from the day of my birth!"

"From even before then," the vagabond interjected.

Konstantin attempted to not miss a beat, though the comment did not sit well with him. "Today, I will walk out on that deck and beg the world for forgiveness for the sins of the Church over two millennia, and promise reforms while dispelling the many myths of supremacy and infallibility—"

"Christopher," the vagabond interrupted. "The Bride of Christ does not... *cannot* sin. Those words that you speak of will never pass your lips."

"Do you bathe in ignorance each morning, fool?" Konstantin had lost any sense of composure at this point. "Look at the Church's history! It has held the world in its strangling clutch of control, teaching whatever it wills to maintain dominion over the consciences of the faithful, restricting their God-given freedoms! Is that what you stand before me defending?"

The vagabond, without the slightest hint of emotion, responded, "It is true, Christopher, that like Christ, who was fully Divine and fully human, so too is His Bride. As His body was subject to all the ills of the flesh, eventually being broken, torn, and nailed to a cross in a very *imperfect* fashion, so too the *members* of the Church provide Her human dimension. They, even leaders, even Popes, have sinned greatly over the centuries—for which forgiveness must be asked. But you must remember, they acted *against* Her Teachings. They, as all of us are at some points, served as cancerous cells in the Body, but they never infected the soul."

Konstantin shook his head in a frustrated fashion. "You are simply splitting hairs to rationalize what you wish to be true."

"Poor Christopher."

"Stop calling me that name!"

The stately man looked upon him with pity—an emotion never before directed at Konstantin in his very privileged life. Yet still it was only the vagabond who spoke. "You have been the pawn of men with an agenda to destroy the very foundation of Christ's Bride since your birth. Your formation and ascension within the hierarchy has been meticulously orchestrated."

"Are you suggesting that I am not legitimately the Supreme Pontiff?" Konstantin bellowed incredulously.

"Quite the contrary, Christopher. In truth, you *are* the successor to Peter, and the Keeper of the Keys to the Kingdom, passed down through Apostolic Succession."

"Another myth," Konstantin responded coldly, though somewhat less emphatically. Hearing that these men *did* believe in the legitimacy of his appointment to this office had let some of the virulence out of his angered spirit.

"Yet despite the plans of men," the vagabond continued, "*Elohim* has spoken for His own purposes, which at times are mysterious. You have been given these Keys, though you will be called upon to relinquish them for a time. One who is an impostor will make claim to your Chair. He will bring about much discord and division in the Body under the guise of unity. But he will not be from the Petrine line."

"So now you are prophets?"

The old vagabond smiled. "We have been in this room before. With this office, you have been granted a gift. It is this gift which will prevent you from carrying out your own tainted will for the Bride of Christ."

Konstantin tried to dismiss the feelings of uncertainty which began to well up within him. All he could muster was a curt, closing response. "We will see, old man."

"And you, Christopher, will be the first-fruits prefigured, for your own motherland."

The sensation of his insides being torn apart was becoming overwhelming. Konstantin winced. "Leave me," he whispered, his voice beginning to quiver.

"There is much personal suffering ahead for you, Christopher, but this will serve to console His Sacred Heart, and to bring about your redemption. We will speak to you again, in the presence of another, in this very room."

Konstantin wrapped his arms about himself, now feeling as if he had fallen headfirst upon the ground, his body bursting open, all his insides pouring out.

"Please... go..."

And with that, the two men were no more to be seen.

A moment passed, and Konstantin felt as if menacing claws released their grip from his very being. He fell prostrate onto the floor, weeping like a child who for the first time felt the loving embrace of his lost mother.

12

"And I saw a great Raven, who was to be a prophet, emerge from a house of noble lineage. He bore the name of division, and in his time, performed countless miracles. Yet his heart was that of unyielding ice. And I saw the Raven kneel before the Beast, and cause others to kneel before him, paying the Beast homage."

– St. Vincent of the Sand (967-996)

i

Vanya cautiously stepped into the café, scanning the room for her father while trying to appear as if she was just taking in the scene. The café was about seven miles outside of town, and Vanya had seized this opportunity as Luther was again away on "business", this time accompanied by Jeffrey. The boys were asleep at home, and per instructions, Vanya had left the audio-visual baby monitor on in their room. She had been informed that one of her father's men would watch the house, also having the necessary equipment to obtain the monitor frequency and unscramble it. Not a very responsible way to supervise infants, but Social Services was the least of her concerns at the moment.

"Go ahead and move to the back table on the left," a voice from behind her whispered, though it was not that of her father. It was...

"Don't look so suspicious, sis. Take it easy and move."

"Yerik?" she inquired as she moved towards the table as instructed.

"Yup, the one and only."

They slid into their respective seats, and Yerik, her younger brother by only eighteen months, reached over and clasped her hand. "It is so good to see you Vannie."

"I can't believe it took you three weeks to track me down. Is Papa getting a little rusty in his old age?"

Yerik looked down.

Vanya suddenly became alarmed. "What is it? Where's Papa?"

Yerik looked back up and sighed. "It's not good, Vannie. Ivankov was indicted last week, and within days Papa was too. He's been indicted on a murder charge and is out right now on bail. He's under the new federal form of house arrest—absolutely no contact with the outside world, save his immediate family and a lawyer. Once a week, he's permitted out, but his movement is monitored and restricted to a ten-mile radius from the house."

Vanya hesitated. "Did he do it?"

Yerik became irritated. "Don't ask me that, Vannie! You *know* better than to ask that. The bottom line is Papa will not be doing any traveling or talking with any of his associates for some time now. Family are the only ones who won't raise suspicion."

"Who's with the boys?"

"Mikhail Ostankino."

"Great, he better not be smoking around them. Are you here alone?"

"Freeman is two tables down. We're safe."

Vanya glanced quickly over to see the man to which her brother referred. She barely got a glance of his profile before he turned away. Vanya vaguely recalled her husband, Gaetano, mentioning the name at one time or another but had never met the man herself.

"He seems kind of nervous."

"Yeah, his wife is about to give birth any minute. Still, he volunteered to help with this—a pretty loyal fella. We needed someone who was not a Ruskie so as to not raise suspicion."

Vanya cocked an eyebrow while Freeman shot a quick glance in her direction. "Yeah, he's about as apple-pie American as you get. Papa's really widening his circle of trust."

"Unfortunately, he does not have much of a choice in these times."

A saddened look came across Vanya's face as she looked down. "How did Papa take the news about Marisha?"

"How do you think?" Yerik bit in, but then softened his tone. "He feels helpless, Vannie. He feels he failed her, and he doesn't want to make the same mistake with you. That's why, when he got your message, he sent me to bring you and his grandchildren back. Ostankino's waiting for my word."

"I can't come back now, and you need to make sure Mikhail doesn't try to move the boys!"

Yerik stared at his sister. "Am I hearing you correctly, Vannie?" His voice began to rise. "Have you lost your mind, like Marisha? God rest her soul!"

"Yerik, keep your voice down!" Vanya scolded.

"Vannie, it has been a year! Mum and Papa have been put through hell! Now we have found you and the kids—we need to leave now!"

"No, Yerik, listen to me, we can't... we..." Vanya was transitioning from argumentative to a thoughtful, persuasive mode. "There is something more at play here, something that could put the boys' lives in danger if we just pick up and leave."

"Trust me, sis. I don't care how extensive this cult is; they won't be able to touch you once you've left. Really, I can't even believe we are discussing this. Let's get the boys and take off. We have this window now!"

"Listen to me!" Vanya pleaded in a harsh whisper. "There is something else going on here! Jesse could die if we just grabbed them and ran!"

"You seem to have inherited a propensity for exaggeration from Mum. The danger is if you stay."

"No, Yerik." Vanya looked up at her brother. Her eyes began to fill with tears. "I don't know what it is, but I don't think the boys can be taken much more than a mile from the home without something very bad happening to them."

Yerik stopped in his tracks, his tone softening. "What do you mean, Vannie?"

"I-I've tried to take the boys out... you know... away from the house." Vanya sniffled, trying to keep herself composed.

"Go on," Yerik muttered, with a stern look on his face.

"Jeffrey was very specific about not taking the children from the neighborhood, but I figured they needed some fresh air and thought it might be a good opportunity to see how closely I was being watched. So I took them out for a long walk in their strollers... it was a terrible mistake to disobey him."

"So what are you telling me, Vannie? He's got some guys shadowing you?"

"No, no, it's more than that, it's..."

"Vannie, Papa's going to have this bastard cut into a million pieces, then we won't have to worry about him period. Do you know Mom is—?"

"Yerik! Would you listen to me? There's more to it than that."

"I'm listening," Yerik said, trying to appear calm.

"When I took the boys out, after about an hour, Jesse began to grab at his ears and scream, then he began to vomit. Before I could do anything, he stopped breathing."

"What?"

"He started wheezing and then just stopped. I started running back towards the home in a panic, and within seconds he began breathing again. We waited for a few minutes, and he was fine. But when I started walking again, in the opposite direction of the house, it happened again."

"Vannie," her brother was shaking his head. "I think you're starting to imagine things. You must—"

"Yerik!" Vanya now looked angry. "I was clueless as to why this was happening. After the third time of trying to move in that direction, a paramedic showed up out of nowhere and instructed me to take the boys home immediately. Three times, Yerik! The same thing happened!"

"So the paramedic was one of *them*?"

Vanya shook her head. "I don't know... maybe... but he made some comment like, 'it is not time'. A little strange, but with all the bizarre stuff going on here, I really didn't take much notice of him."

"So what are you saying then, Vannie? Is it a satanic hex?" Yerik asked, not fully masking his hint of sarcasm.

"I'm saying that the boy stops breathing when he gets more than a mile from our house, Yerik... call it a hex, call it whatever, I don't care... these people are into a lot of things, including science-medical stuff. It could be something much less... less *spiritual*... like an implant or something. But until I can find out what's going on, the boys are not going anywhere!"

Yerik hesitated, seeing the determination in Vanya's eyes. "Vannie, I can't go back and face Papa without you. What would I tell him?"

"Tell him I have more legwork to do before we try anything. I want out too, trust me. I know I can learn more, and when I find a way around this 'hex' or whatever it is, I'll be contacting Papa immediately. I can handle Jeffrey, and I can deal with Luther. These men are Satanists, I am sure of that, though they never describe themselves as such. And Luther has some peculiar but protective interest in Jesse."

"This isn't sitting well with me, Vannie." Yerik leaned closer to her and spoke in a more nervous tone. "I need to tell you, Vannie, it is very likely that Papa needs to get out of the country, and he won't leave without you and his grandkids. Our window is brief; he seems to think this charge will not go away. He won't leave without you! And if he stays, well, the D.A. has already made it clear that he will seek the death penalty."

"Jesus, Mary, and Joseph."

"What can I tell him?"

Vanya put her head in her hands. "Lord, help us. I would love nothing more than to drive away from this place with the boys today. But at best, we will blow my cover if we have to turn back because of Jesse. At worst, we could be killing the last part of Marisha left on this Earth."

They sat and just stared at each other, holding back tears of hopelessness, as the spirit called despair slowly wrapped his venomous tentacles around them.

ii

Luther stood at the altar with the seven Arch-Ministers of the Brotherhood of the Coming Prince. The Grand Elder, the Highest of High Priests, lay in the middle of their circle on a stone slab, gasping for what would be his final breaths on this plane of existence.

Though Luther had not risen to the ranks of Arch-Minister, he had been Spiritual Apprentice to the Grand Elder since the age of twelve when he had been brought into the Brotherhood. Though no one dared ask, it was rumored that he had been placed under the guidance of the Grand Elder by the *Illumini*.

The *Illumini* themselves were never seen, never heard, and rarely mentioned for fear of dire repercussions. The existence of the *Illumini* was not even an established certainty. But the thought of this Council made each of the Arch-Ministers feel as if he was head of a cheap sideshow.

"What are we to do?" questioned Thaaoth, Arch-Minister of Africa. "He was the first, the only, and we have no means of succession!"

"The Master will guide us!" spoke Galaas, Arch-Minister of Western Asia. "We must follow His will!"

"The Master has already spoken." It was Luther who addressed the group this time.

All members of the Supreme Council looked towards him in incredulity, if not irritation. Luther turned his back on the altar and walked towards the ancient symbol of their kind engraved on the floor. The Council waited for Luther to speak further, but he did not offer any more. Finally, the Arch-Minister of Europe spoke up.

"Father Luther?"

"Yes, Lord Gethog?"

The Arch-Minister cleared his throat, attempting to present himself authoritatively. "Could you please enlighten the rest of us on your...your vision?"

"Indeed I shall. The Master is revolted by our spineless leadership. He has grown wearisome of multiple factions in His name. We have become divided out of feebleness, not unlike the Christians!"

"Father Luther!" It was Horlon, Arch-Minister of South America, speaking in a disgusted tone. The teardrop-shaped birthmark under his left eye, piggybacking on his facial contortions of distaste, presented a macabre picture to the group. "Remember your place! Do you suggest that the Grand Elder is—?"

"Was," Luther said solemnly.

"What do you mean *was*? As long as there is breath in his—"

Luther closed his eyes and clenched his jaw. He inhaled deeply, then slowly let the breath out, murmuring something inaudible to the others. The Highest of High Priests took one last, violent gasp and then retired.

The members of the Supreme Council looked at each other, and then back to Luther in disbelief.

"What... have.... you... DONE?" Horlon snapped, barely able to control himself.

"*I* have done nothing. However, the Master has enacted His will through me," Luther responded, only now opening his eyes.

"What do *you* know of The Master's will?" Horlon pursued with a touch of sarcasm in his voice.

"You doubt me." Luther was now facing Horlon. "Not only that, you seek to discredit me! As do you, Lord Innon, and you, Lord Aaoth!"

Luther glared at each of them as he spoke.

"I have foreseen what will come to pass. You will find that our Grand Elder did establish a right of succession in his *Book of Shadows*. We will abide by his enlightened will in this matter. But be assured of this; we will be unable to choose a successor for seventy-four cycles. This has been foretold to me, as there will be great division among us."

"Since you have your own direct line to the Master, why do you not just let us in on His will and save us all the trouble, Luther?" It was Arch-Minister Galethog, the head of the Brotherhood in the Far East speaking, with a heavy note of contempt in his voice.

Luther smiled and closed his eyes. "Ye of such little faith. In the end, there will be only one choice, the Master's choice. And this man will be the Great Prophet, for the latter days are at hand."

"I will not stand for this nonsense!" shouted Horlon. "Yes, we will read the *Book of Shadows*, as it is only logical that the Grand Elder would have written his thoughts on succession there. But as for this ranting of a certifiable deranged lunatic, I have no place for it!"

Horlon turned to leave but froze in his steps at the chilling tone of Luther's voice.

"Lord Horlon."

Why can't I move my feet?

"Shall death have no dominion?"

13

Close the door, put out the light
No They won't be home tonight
The snow falls hard, and don't you know?
The winds of Thor are blowing cold

They're wearing steel that's bright and true
They carry news that must get through
They choose a path where no one goes.

– Led Zeppelin
No Quarter

i

Weeks moved into months and months moved into years. While Vanya was able to maintain somewhat of a status quo, raising Tobias and Jesse with faithful diligence, it was like walking a tightrope above a sea of fire. She had not been able to solve the riddle of Jesse's invisible prison. She learned that she too was being monitored, as she had to answer for her clandestine meeting with her brother. She was able to deflect any more serious attention by "admitting" that she met up with an old flame of hers, promising it would never happen again.

Her father remained under tight surveillance and had been unable to come up with a plan that would guarantee the ongoing safety of both children. The powerlessness he was now experiencing was unprecedented in his life. But a step outside of the perimeter of his yard (or the once a week excursion within the court-dictated ten-mile radius of his home) would ensure the revocation of his bail, and then he would be of no help to anyone. For Nesterov's part, despite his family sentiments, at this juncture he felt the discovery of the mole in his syndicate was top priority. As additional indictments began to be handed down on other members, it was clear that this person was still active.

Their grim predicament notwithstanding, today, however, would be a day of celebration. It was the twin's fifth birthday. But as usual, it was really only a celebration for Tobias. Jeffrey had planned the entire festive event, where all of Tobias' friends would come and participate in a good time. Jesse, on the other hand, was required to remain in his room.

Jeffrey had grown tired of seeing Jesse's face, so he set up a separate "bedroom" for him in a hallway walk-in closet. Jesse could hear the party downstairs and sat in the middle of his room quietly weeping. He had learned not to cry out loud, for this would most certainly result in a beating from his father.

Wrapped in his own solitude, Jesse heard footsteps coming up the stairs.

He heard me crying! he thought, suddenly terrified.

He quickly huddled against the back corner of the room, pulling himself into the fetal position. There was a knock at his door.

Daddy don't knock, he thought. Still, he was too terrified to speak.

"Jes?" it was his brother's voice.

"Toby? Is that you?" Excitement snuck into the words escaping from Jesse's vocal chords.

The door opened and Tobias entered, hiding something behind his back.

Jesse's countenance brightened. This was Tobias, the brother who would always look out for him when his father came home drunk. Tobias, who took the blame when Jesse had carved their names in their nanny's harpsichord. Tobias, who he knew more than anything else, he loved.

"Toby! Why aren't you at your party?"

"Aww, it's really not that fun. Just Daddy acting silly in front of the guys."

Jesse looked down. It hurt enough that his father treated him so horribly. But to know that his father could be so wonderful to perfect strangers was like a dagger in the heart.

"Hey, Jes, I got somethin' for ya."

"What?" Jesse had the spark back in his eye.

"Here."

Tobias pulled out a piece of birthday cake from behind his back. Jesse's face lit up at the sight of his brother's gift. As he reached for it, however, his eyes dropped and a sad look came over his face.

"Daddy's gonna get me if I do."

"No way, Jes! I grabbed the piece and then said I had to go pee. Daddy doesn't know anything!"

Jesse smiled and accepted the gift from his brother. Tobias had even brought him a plastic fork.

"I gotta go before Daddy comes looking. Bye, Jes!"

Jesse looked up with chocolate already smudged on his face. No matter how bad things got, his brother always came though for him.

"Thanks, Toby."

ii

"Good evening, Dr. Dylan."

Kate Thomas was barely able to pull her eyes away from the flat-screen television propped up above the nurses' station. It was President Amarab's second State of the Union address in his third term as Commander in Chief. It was clearly for the good of the country that Senator William Maison had pushed through a Constitutional Amendment nearly three years back. The Amendment first gave people the right to re-elect a president for more than two terms, and second, it modified Article II of the Constitution, making eligibility for the office of president fully inclusive, ending the discriminating practices that barred many from the post. It passed by a narrow margin, (bigotry, unfortunately, was still alive and well) but the Amendment *was* necessary—prosperity seemed just around the corner, and this was definitely the man to do it.

"Good evening, Kate. How are my patients doing?"

Kate finally diverted her eyes from the television.

"Oh, the usual. 13B continues to wet his bed on purpose. Says the FBI checks the sewage lines in order to get a urine sample. 14A still insists that she's Elvis' child after he made it with a Martian lady, and 2B continues to chide me on the cost-effectiveness of this place. Like I said, same-old same-old."

Dr. Dylan chuckled. Nurse Thomas had quite the gift of sarcastic humor, which he knew was almost a necessity for such a job. Still, his smile slowly faded, being replaced by a look of discomfort.

"What about...?"

"Please, Doctor, I'd rather not even think about it. I check on him once a day to see if he's still breathing. And to be honest, I pray each time that maybe he's not. But he's still hanging in there. I just don't get it." Kate was starting to quiver.

"Has he eaten anything?"

"No, Doctor. Not today, not yesterday, not last week, not last year. Doc, be straight with me. Is this some government experiment or something? How the hell is that man alive?"

Dr. Dylan shook his head. He had been asking himself that same question for nearly five years. Room 6F was one he was not too fond of visiting either. This man, if he could even be called that, was found just wandering around the city with no clothes, no hair, no teeth, not even any fingernails remaining to speak of. Yet he was still able to gouge the eyes out of the first unfortunate officer that attempted to subdue him. He didn't eat. He didn't sleep. He just bounced around his room like a raving lunatic and then sat mumbling the same phrase to himself over and over again.

"Doctor?" It was Kate speaking. "Doctor, are you all right?"

Dr. Dylan shook the brief reverie he had fallen into from his consciousness. "I...uh...I'm sorry, Kate. I've got a lot on my mind. I'm going to go back and take a look."

"Suit yourself." Kate's look was one of slight suspicion, not having received an answer to her question. She was sure this was some kind of government experiment, with its natural subsequent conspiracy for a cover-up. Still, if it took place on President Amarab's watch, there was certainly good justification for it. She mused on the thought only a moment longer before turning her attention back to the presidential address.

Dr. Dylan walked down corridor F. He was thinking about moving the subject to the last door on the hallway, thereby reducing the need to pass his room with any frequency. He had even thought of moving him off the sixth floor altogether. But in the end, Dr. Dylan determined that moving him at all could potentially prove more hazardous than the trouble was worth. As for now, the subject was secure, and heck, there was no reason to open the door. They had given up trying to feed him months ago. If this went on much longer, he would seek a court order to euthanize the man.

Shouldn't be too hard. Who would argue that this wasn't a miserable existence?

Dr. Dylan looked in the small view window to room 6F. As he had done countless times before, he watched curiously as the burn and claw marks appeared on the subject's body. The subject screamed in agony, then within minutes the marks were gone. He knew they would be replaced shortly—they always were.

What the hell is this thing?

Dr. Dylan felt the familiar sense of nausea begin to rise within him. He was about to turn away when the subject spotted him, leapt forward and slammed up against the view window. His one identifying mark, a teardrop-shaped birthmark under his left eye, seemed to glow a pale green hue. He stood there for a moment, staring deeply into the eyes of his doctor, then slumped to the floor, mumbling the same thing over and over again.

"And death *shall* have dominion... and death *shall* have dominion..."

iii

"This is ludicrous! We have been bucking this procedure going on five years now!" bellowed the hefty Lord Innon. "We must settle for a majority vote!"

"But that would be against the will of the Grand Elder. He was very specific in his *Book of Shadows* that it must be a unanimous vote," interrupted Lord Gethog.

"We've been in a three to three deadlock for the last thirteen meetings. It's not going to change!" retorted Innon.

"These things take time," Luther stated with just a trace of a sneer on his face.

Innon slammed the table and leaned forward aggressively to within six inches of Luther' face.

"We are just about out of *time*, Luther. Our following is dwindling. They are crying for leadership. We have given them nothing, so we stand to lose everything!"

Luther slowly rose from his seat, his eyes fixed on those of Innon. With each passing cycle, the Arch-Ministers had grown more frustrated and restless, which paradoxically caused Luther to become more calm and secure. He glanced at each member of the Supreme Council, then back at Innon before saying calmly, "You are a fool, Innon. While you worry about the loss of a few heathens, I see the day when our flock expands one hundred fold—the day when people will gladly tear their hearts out to become one with us. The day will come where *all* men will bow to the Master!"

Innon was seething. He did not take kindly to being called a fool. "I am sick of your rhetoric, Luther! You obviously feel that you will be chosen as successor to the Grand Elder over the Brotherhood when you do not even carry the majority vote! I am not afraid of you, Luther, and though I cannot prove it, I know you had something to do with what happened to Lord Horlon. You will never get my vote, so you will never receive a unanimous decision. You hear me? You will never get my vote!"

There was a deafening quiet in the room. Only after what seemed like hours did Luther break the silence.

"I never asked for your vote, *Lord* Innon."

14

Allied Press ~

KHARTOUM - A recent International Red Cross study, released on Thursday, identifies the current H-virus Positive rate in Sub-Saharan Africa to be 37%. This figure is up 13% from only five years ago. Uganda remains the only African nation where the rate continues to decline.

To date, 107 mutations of the H-virus have been identified, further reducing the likelihood of a vaccine within the next ten years. Scientists have had some minimal success in eliminating three forms of the H-virus but admit that the virus is now mutating at a rate faster than their research can keep up with.

A special emergency meeting of the United Nations will be held this Wednesday to discuss the possibility of an international quarantine of all countries identified in the study.

The study still has the worldwide H-virus rate holding at 21%.

SEED

i

Jesse had snuck into Tobias' bedroom before. It was really the only opportunity he had to spend time alone with his brother. Sure, Nanny Vanya would teach him and Tobias to pray, saying the "Our Father" and "Hail Mary" together, but he wanted to play with his brother too.

His Nanny Vanya had said that now he and Tobias were five, they would get to receive something called "first communion". They would be sneaking out tomorrow after their father left, and Jesse wanted to check with his brother to make sure he knew everything to do.

"Toby?" he whispered.

There was a rustling in the sheets.

"Jes?" a sleepy Tobias inquired.

"I forgot what to say tomorrow."

Tobias sat up in his bed, shaking some of the sleepiness from his head, and smiled.

"Come on up."

Jesse smiled and hopped up onto Tobias' bed. It was nice to be sitting on a real mattress with a real box spring instead of a large bag stuffed with old clothes.

"What did you forget, Jes?" Tobias asked his brother.

"Well," Jesse began. "D'ya know when you walk up to the front with your hands folded. Ya know, up to the griest?"

"Priest, Jes, priest."

"Yeah that's what I meant, the priest. Well, he says something to you before I get that piece of bread, and I'm s'posed to say something back, like 'thanks' or somethin', right?"

Tobias started to laugh and had to cover his mouth. He stopped immediately when he saw that he had hurt his brother's feelings. Jesse was so fragile! Anyway, he managed to quickly change his expression.

"Sorry, Jes, I was just tickling myself. You tell the priest 'A-Men'. That's all."

"And I'm allowed to stick my tongue out at him?"

Tobias smiled, but he did not laugh this time.

"Yeah, but only for a sec."

"Okay."

"But, Jes, you gotta remember, it's not bread, it's Jesus. He loves us and wants to come into us and be in our hearts."

"Does Jesus love me?"

Tobias' eyes widened, "Yeah He does! He loves everybody!"

Jesse's eyes filled up. "Then why does He let Daddy be mean to me?"

Tobias was silent for the moment. "I-I am not sure, Jes. I think that makes Him sad too."

A look of grave sadness crept over Jesse's face. "Do you think I'm not going to be able to breathe this time, Toby?"

Tobias too felt a certain grief, but he knew he could not let his brother see this. "No way, Jes, we're only going a little way this time, not real far like that time we were playing."

Jesse looked up at his brother, obviously dwelling on that horrible incident when he and Tobias had disobeyed Nanny Vanya and gone out exploring.

"Besides, Jes," Tobias continued, "Nanny Vanya says that 'If God is for us, who can be against?'"

That was all it took. In an instant Jesse was smiling again. "Your bed feels real good. I wish I had one too!" he exclaimed.

"Here, lie down. There's enough room," Tobias instructed.

"But Daddy will—"

"Only for a second, Jes, then you can go back before Daddy wakes up."

"All right, just for a sec."

Jesse lay down on his brother's pillow and thought that he felt more relaxed than he ever had in his entire life. One day he would get himself a bed like this, he just knew it. It felt so good, maybe he could close his eyes just for a second to see how it would feel. Then he might... he might...

Jesse could not fully discern at exactly what point he was fully awake, but he was already aware of an intense pain in his nose and warm blood filling his nostrils.

"You bastard son of a bitch!"

As the second blow came down on the side of his head, Jesse could recognize his father's voice.

"Daddy, I'm sorry... I'm—"

Jeffrey had now yanked Jesse out of the bed by his hair and slammed him against the wall. "What the hell do you think you're doing in here with my son?"

"Daddy, stop! It was my idea! I told him to!" It was Tobias' terrified voice screaming this time, which caused a brief break in the action. Jeffrey turned towards Tobias, holding Jesse six inches off the ground by his neck.

"Son, please excuse yourself for a minute. I need to teach Jesse some respect."

"But Daddy, I—"

Jeffrey gave Tobias a look that made it clear any discussion was over. Tobias fled the scene and ran into Vanya's room. Vanya jumped up as the door burst open.

"Nanny Vanya!" he yelped in a petrified voice. "Daddy's hurting Jesse!"

Vanya could now hear the screaming and intermittent thuds. She jumped from her bed and raced down the hall, praying silently while screaming aloud, "MR. CHARDIN, STOP THIS!"

She ran into the room to find Jeffrey picking Jesse up off the floor by his collar. He was raising his fist as a terrified Jesse looked on.

"STOP!" she screamed in a tone which could not be dismissed.

Jeffrey looked over. He was panting and had the fire of the devil in his eyes.

"Stay out of this, Vanya." His rage had lessened only a margin. "I need to teach this boy that there are consequences for disobeying me."

Though Jeffrey was in charge of the house, he deliberately avoided confrontations with Vanya. As Luther had reflected to him, there was something about her that was...*disquieting*.

"Let the boy go," Vanya spoke firmly, clenching her jaw.

Jesse was weeping silently; his head drooped down with Jeffrey still holding him above the floor. Jeffrey released his grip, and Jesse fell flat. He looked down upon Jesse, then back at Vanya, clearing the hair out of his eyes. "You stay away from my son, you little bastard!" he snapped, giving Jesse one last kick.

Jeffrey walked to leave the room, attempting to give Vanya one last intimidating stare. It did not work. He looked away quickly and moved out of the bedroom. Jesse began to cry out loud now.

Vanya moved over to the bed and wrapped her arms around him. "Oh, my little Jesse, I'm sorry. I'm so sorry."

Jesse attempted to sniffle back his bleeding, runny nose. "He hates me! W-Why does he hate me?"

"He doesn't hate you, Jesse. He's afraid of you."

Jesse stopped sniffling and looked up at Vanya.

"A-Afraid of me?"

"Yes, Jesse, afraid," Vanya continued. "From the day I laid eyes on you, and heard the name your mumma had given you, I knew you were something special. I knew that you would grow up to be a very important person one day, and that's what frightens your stepfather."

Jesse sniffled, trying to absorb the confusing information that Vanya was providing him. "Tell me more about my mumma, Nanny Vanya."

"Yes, I will, Jesse, but you mustn't tell anyone."

"What was she like?" Jesse inquired.

"What was Marisha like?" Vanya was now pondering, looking off into space. "Marisha, your mumma, was what you call a free spirit."

Jesse's eyes widened. "Like the Holy Spirit?"

Vanya restrained herself from chuckling.

"No, not quite, Jesse. Your mumma enjoyed each and every moment of her life, even when things were going bad, because she always did exactly what she wanted to do, no matter what anyone else thought. And right up to the moment she returned to God, she loved you, Jesse, with all her heart."

Jesse got teary-eyed again. "Daddy says I killed her!"

This hit Vanya hard, and she had to struggle from gasping. What some people would say to children! "That's not true, Jesse! Don't you believe that for a second! Jesus called your mumma home because He loved her so much that He couldn't stand not having her with Him right then and there!"

Jesse managed a slight smile through his tear-stained face.

"Nanny Vanya?"

"Yes, Jesse?"

"Do you know who my real daddy is?"

A troubled look crept across Vanya's face. No, she did not know for sure who Jesse's father was, but she could not dismiss the way Luther gazed at Jesse. It was like a child looking at an ice cream. A shiver ran through her body before she managed to push the thought out of her mind.

"God in Heaven is the Father of us all, Jesse," she replied, hoping this would be sufficient.

It wasn't. Jesse produced a frown. "You know what I mean, Nanny Vanya," he prodded.

At this point, Tobias walked in sheepishly.

"Jes, I'm sorry I let you fall asleep. I'm sorry Daddy hit you. Please don't hate me."

Vanya smiled sadly, held her arms out and instantly the three of them were hugging.

"I know what we can do to cheer each other up!" Vanya spoke in an excited tone.

Jesse looked up with a gleeful expression. "The harp-i-corn!"

Vanya was smiling. "Harpsichord, Jesse."

The brothers sprinted out of the room as Vanya slowly walked downstairs. The two were already sitting on the bench in front of the harpsichord, leaving a space between them for Vanya. She stepped over the bench and sat down, enjoying the look of anticipation in the boys' eyes. Many times she had turned their tears to joy with the simple instrument, a piano that plucked strings instead of striking them with a hammer. What a beautiful sound it made.

Vanya began to play a selection from Bach, her favorite composer and harpsichord virtuoso. She watched Tobias' look of delight as he smiled and wiggled along to the tune she was playing. But Jesse's reaction was always quite different. He maintained a faint smile on his face as he closed his eyes, dreaming. Though he was physically right there with her, Vanya sensed his consciousness floating an eternity away. At these moments he was someplace wonderful, someplace peaceful, and she always felt a touch of sadness when she completed her piece and had to make Jesse to return from his place of tranquility to such a cold and harsh reality.

Things were happening. Things were changing. But Vanya did not allow herself to dare ponder whether they would be for the better or worse.

ii

Alexandre Nesterov sat in front of the fireplace staring at the flames. A nearly empty glass of Wild Turkey was on a small table to his left (Nesterov was perhaps the *only* Russian who did not have a taste for Vodka), and on the table to his right sat a loaded pistol.

"I have failed. Failed as a father, failed as a husband," he spoke openly to the flames, mesmerized, feeling some strange sense that they understood him.

"*Yessss.... You have failed...*"

"I command so many men, yet I cannot even protect my own children."

"*You are weak...*"

The licks, crackles and pops spoke so... so clearly.

"I was unable to save my own daughter, my baby girl."

"*You drove her away... she had no choice... she went to her grave hating you...*"

"And now, Vanya. She is smart, but such a fool. She thinks she can handle these things. She does not know what she is dealing with."

"*Nor do you... you are as lost as she... and you have no power to change what is about to happen...*"

"What?" Nesterov jolted. "What is about to happen?"

"*You will stand at their graves... and your woman will hate you for eternity for it!*"

A loud pop, and the flames seemed to grow in grandeur and power.

"I cannot leave this place! I cannot command! I cannot get to my daughter and grandchildren! I can trust no one!"

"There is no way out... except one..."

Nesterov's eyes widened, then moved to where the flames directed, slowly fixing on the pistol.

"Alexandre?" A voice emerged from beyond the shadows, along with a banging on a door.

"Take the woman with you! Then end this! Move to the next journey! This one is lost!"

"Alexandre! Who are you talking to? Open this door!"

"I-I..."

"Do not listen to her! She led you to this! End this NOW!"

Nesterov turned to the door, then glanced back at the pistol. His head began to swim.

"What... what am I...?" he reached towards the door from his seat.

"Do not go deeper into this weakness, you pathetic fool!"

"Annie, Annie, help... help me!"

"I promise you an eternity of endless rooms of darkness and misery if you fail me now!"

"Alex! Oh my God!"

Nesterov's hand lay gripped on the pistol as he began to lift it, fighting an instinct to point it towards the door, drawing it towards his temple.

Two thousand miles away, Vanya played away on the harpsichord as Jesse, lost in some other world, breathed the word, *"Grandpa—"*

Father Daniel Ananias, praying fervently before the tabernacle, experienced an intense shooting pain through his head. He gasped for breath as he slumped to the floor.

The bullet went straight into the fireplace and ricocheted, exploding the glass of Wild Turkey, then shattering the family picture on the wall, finally imbedding itself in the thick support beam on the far side of the room. The fire flared for a moment, then extinguished as Annie D. was finally able to burst into the room through the jammed door that had no lock. She clutched a rosary in her hand.

She caught Alexandre as he fell forward. The man who sent fear into the heart of thousands trembled in her arms, breaking into the sobs of one who had lost all hope.

15

"By the pricking of my thumbs,
Something wicked this way comes.

Open, locks,
Whoever knocks!"

– Second Witch
Macbeth

i

Lord Innon sat in the far corner of The Cloven Hoof restaurant sipping his wine and looking coolly around the room. He did not put it beyond Luther to have his people follow him from place to place. However, in his self-absorbed arrogance, Innon assured himself that he had outwitted Luther on this occasion. He stuffed another handful of peanuts into his mouth.

The near-anorexic Lord Aaoth entered the front of the restaurant. Despite the mild weather and late hour, he was clad in a dark trench coat and sunglasses.

What an idiot, Innon mused.

Aaoth spotted Innon, nodded in his direction and moved quickly towards the table. He removed his trench coat and gave the room its third once-over before removing his glasses. He sat down and immediately began to speak in an edgy fashion.

"This is totally insane, Innon! You know meeting outside of the

Conclave is forbidden! If we get caught—"

"Your cowardice is sickening," Innon chided. "What we are meeting about is of much greater importance than any petty fears you might have. We are here to prevent the destruction of our Brotherhood. What could be a more noble purpose?"

Aaoth winced at the sound of Innon's chastising tone and then slowly slipped into a foreboding sense of despair. He was a pawn, and he knew it. Being Arch-Minister for Australia was no great feat. In fact, it was by far the smallest region in the Brotherhood. Still, he was firm in his belief that Luther should not assume the position of Grand Elder, the Highest of High Priests. That was, of course, unless he had to stand alone. At this point, he and Innon were the only men remaining who stood between Luther and that position.

"Listen, Brother Innon," Aaoth spoke, trying to sound assertive. "I'll do what you say, I'll support you for as long as I can, but I am not going to take the fall for you, or for anybody for that matter." He hesitated, looking for a response from Innon. Receiving none, he anxiously continued, "So what is it you have in mind?"

Aaoth was beginning to develop some perspiration above his lip. Innon was somewhat amused at his attempt at being potent.

"It would be good for you to relax, Brother Aaoth, all has been arranged."

Aaoth looked confused.

"What do you mean 'all has been arranged?'"

Innon looked over several tables and nodded to a man sitting alone. The man got up from his table and began walking towards them. He was a rather large individual—even larger than Innon—being well over six feet tall and probably weighing in the neighborhood of two hundred and fifty pounds. The man, despite his size, moved gracefully across the room, sitting down to Innon's right.

"Lord Aaoth," Innon announced, "meet Bartholomew Justus, the answer to all of our problems."

Aaoth was too astonished to speak. Bartholomew Justus reached across the table to shake his hand, revealing a large tattoo of the Virgin Mary on his inner forearm. His breath carried the stench of a recently smoked cigar.

"Pleased to meet you, Mr. Aaoth."

Aaoth did not offer his hand to Justus. Instead he turned his look of amazement to Innon. "Are you out of your mind?" Aaoth was not acting this time. "A...a hit man? The Mafia? Even worse, a Catholic?"

Justus jumped in before Innon could respond. "Pardon my bluntness, Mr. Aaoth, but I don't give a damn what your religion is, what kind of car you drive, or who—" Aaoth winced at the crassness of this man's continued monologue. "—and for your information, I'm not involving my benefactor in this. This is a side job I'm doing on my own because Mr. Innon here asked me so nicely. I do a job, and I get paid. Nothing personal."

Aaoth again found himself speechless. His gaze went back and forth between Innon and Justus as if he was watching a tennis match.

Innon broke the uncomfortable silence. "Listen, Brother Aaoth, in two more lunar cycles we will hit the seventy-fifth meeting of the Conclave. This was when Luther predicted we would select a leader, and I feel that he will stop at nothing to make this so-called prophecy become a reality. We need to make our move before he does. You remember what he did to Brother Horlon, don't you?"

Aaoth was looking down, trying to stop shaking.

"Yes."

"Well, I don't know how he did it, but he did. I am sure of that. With you and me out of the way, he would have his unanimous decision. Don't you see that there would be no room for us in his Brotherhood?"

"But it has been said that he is *Illumini*!"

This time it was Innon who winced. "You have listened to too many fairy tales, Aaoth. There is no such group!"

Aaoth looked up at Innon with a mild look of contempt. The twenty-one Apostles of the Great Seraph was more than just a fairy tale, at least so he believed. Aaoth glanced at Justus and then back to Innon.

"The *Illumini*. That has forever been a teaching of our—"

"I am not interested in such things," Lord Innon interrupted, more than a bit irritated. "The truth is, Aaoth, I do not know that I believe in any of it. I believe in power. I believe in having the freedom to harm no one, and do as thou wilt. Sure, if you want to call the embodiment of unfettered self-determination 'the Master', I can live with that. But some cosmic battle between good and evil? Give me a break. The spirit of the antichrist is simply the true spirit of anti-mythology. Nothing more, nothing less."

Aaoth was speechless. Justus tried to hide a smirk from his potential benefactor.

"Listen, Aaoth, I know you're a believer, and that's fine. But we both have the same end in mind, which puts us on the same side. We're either both in it, or we don't do it at all. It's your call."

Aaoth looked up, still trying to conceal his trembling. He looked to Justus, who this time did not even attempt to conceal his grin. Looking down again, he mumbled something that was inaudible to the other two men.

"What?" Innon interrupted. "What was that?"

Aaoth glanced up, a fierce look of anger in his eyes.

"I said, let's do it!"

ii

Vanya was lost. She had not seen this place before and could not remember how she had gotten here. She saw sand surrounding her for miles and miles with burning heaps of mangled metal scattered throughout the scene. Smoke rose above the horizon to a moon which glowed blood red.

In the distance, Vanya could hear the sounds of battle. Voices crying out in pain echoed through her ears. As she continued to absorb the macabre scene, out of nowhere a lamb approached her, bleating like a petrified child. It moved back several steps, then turned to Vanya again with longing eyes. It seemed to beckon to her.

The lamb ran to the top of the sand dune with Vanya following. She reached the top, and then looked down upon an altar, on which limped a dove whose wing was obviously broken. Surrounding the altar were a number of small, decaying animals. Vanya looked down to see a baby rabbit lying at her feet, having obviously been killed recently as it had not yet begun to decompose. She felt an odd sense of connection with the animal, an ominous sense of sadness. Suddenly Vanya heard—she *felt*—a presence behind her, but she was unable to turn around.

"The time for deliverance is at hand," the voice resonated, *"but these things must first come to pass."*

Vanya felt a growing sorrow emanate from inside of her as she watched the dove attempt to fly away from the altar. She tried to move forward but was unable to do so. The dove suddenly ceased its struggle and looked directly up at Vanya.

Their eyes locked. A look of yearning passed right through Vanya, and she found herself crying. Its eyes were human. Its eyes held feeling. The dove would not release its gaze.

Then, with the speed of a jackal, a beast broke forth from the earth behind the altar, and with a single swipe of its claws it ended what little life the dove had left, devouring it in one swallow.

Vanya instantly broke out of her trance and instinctively grabbed the lamb, now screaming, up in her arms. The devouring beast looked up at her, and upon setting eyes on the lamb let out an angry roar which shook the ground. Vanya immediately turned to run.

It began to snow as she fled from the scene, still clutching the lamb in her arms. The snowfall became heavier and heavier until she came to a horrible realization. These were not snowflakes—they were the feathers of a dove.

Another roar bellowed out from behind her. She could feel the breath of the beast upon her. Vanya was now in a full downpour of rain, only it wasn't rain—it was blood. She cried out.

"JESUS!"

In the last instant before the vision broke, she heard the first voice speak again.

"Prepare Ye, for flight! The time is at hand!"

iii

Jesse looked up at the night sky with tears in his eyes. It was another full moon. Tonight, he would again be visited by Luther. He moved away from the window and began walking to his closet.

For as long as he could remember, Luther would visit him on each full moon. He did not know at what time, only that everyone else seemed to be asleep when it happened. He had wanted so badly to tell Tobias, his Nanny Vanya, or even his step-dad about it, but Luther had assured Jesse that whoever he told would die a horrible death.

To prove his point, Luther would occasionally bring along some small animal and whisper to it about the "naughty touches" which he and Jesse were doing. He would then set the animal down, cover Jesse's mouth to muffle his cries, and together they would watch the animal slowly, and no doubt painfully, die.

This was a secret Jesse could never share. He was six now, and though what Luther did to him with his clothes off would hurt, many times even causing him to bleed, Jesse felt that he probably deserved it.

The lonely tears began to stream down Jesse's cheeks as he heard the unmistakable sound of the front door opening. He stood up in his closet and began to remove his clothes, all but his underwear. Luther would remove these during the beginning of the ritual, once the candles had been lit, and the wine had been shared.

Jesse heard the soft footsteps of someone climbing the stairs. His breathing quickened as the footsteps stopped at his door.

Chills shot through him as the familiar three soft yet deliberate knocks rattled his soul.

The next sound Jesse heard could have been easily mistaken for the wind.

"Jessssssssssseeeeeeeeeeee."

The door to his closet opened and Luther's head appeared. His grin sent shivers throughout Jesse's body.

"Good evening, my son."

Jesse felt himself slipping away.

"Good evening, Father."

Luther closed his eyes, inhaling through his nose, savoring the word 'Father' spoken from Jesse's lips.

"I brought you a friend tonight."

Jesse's eyes widened in dread as Luther reached his cupped hands out and opened them not more than a foot from his face. Jesse could not hold back from crying this time after seeing what Luther held in his hands.

It was a baby rabbit.

16

Allied Press   ~

THE VATICAN — After nearly three months of extensive searching, Vatican officials have officially called off the search for the missing airliner that carried Pope Leo XIV. Reportedly, over 5 million square miles of the Atlantic Ocean were included in the search, in which representatives of seventy-two nations participated.

Leo's ascension to the highest office in the Catholic Church was both colorful and unlikely. His predecessor, Christopher I, had his election declared "illegitimate and null" according to a Senate of Cardinals who met in the City of Toulouse. Christopher had stunned the world in his first words as Pope, declaring "Ex-Cathedra" the so-called Fifth Marian Dogma, and then calling on all Bishops in the world to unite with him to "Consecrate Russia to the Immaculate Heart of Mary."

After it was discovered that the secret balloting had been tampered with by members of the Russian GRU, the Senate declared all statements by Christopher to be invalid, then subsequently enforced the measure of excommunication upon the unrepentant cleric. After the cardinals governed the Church collectively for nine months, Marcel Cloison, a French Cardinal, emerged in a manner still contested by some hardliners to be elected Pope Leo XIV.

Leo was beloved both within and outside of the Catholic Church for the reforms introduced during his brief tenure, which rallied the Catholic Church to its highest membership and participation rate ever. The Pontiff would have turned sixty-seven this month.

DOMINION

> There is still no report regarding exactly why the Pontiff was flying over the Atlantic, nor any information regarding his destination. There had been no announcement by the Vatican of any overseas trips scheduled for Pope Leo within the next six weeks.
>
> Roman Catholic cardinals from across the globe are expected to gather in the Vatican over the next few days for the Papal Conclave to choose a successor to their highest-ranking member of the priesthood.

i

Bartholomew Justus took pride in his ability to "off" people in a quick, clean, and discreet manner. He had gotten over the excitement of "shoot-em-up" hits years ago, developing quite a reputation for himself since. After a brief period of engaging in mostly independent contract work, he had finally been taken under the wing of the Caputo family. Now, with the alliance formed between Caputo and the Russian syndicate, his hard work had earned him the position of junior lieutenant to the number two Russian mob boss in the entire country, Alexandre Nesterov.

However, this hit had nothing to do with his ties to the Caputo family, nor with Nesterov for that matter. This was strictly a side job, as things had been somewhat slow and quiet while Nesterov was coping with a murder indictment. He was certain that Mr. Nesterov would have his innards in a jar if he knew what his number one hit man was doing, but being hundreds of miles from Nesterov or Caputo territory, Justus felt safe.

He parked his car about a quarter-mile from the home of his soon-to-be victim and stuck his half-completed cigar into the ashtray. Easing out of his vehicle, Justus slid the eighteen inches of chain-link into his coat pocket. He experienced a slight bit of unease, but this was nothing new. Justus fed off this fear (though he would never identify it as such), which for him was the excitement of the hunt.

He walked along the dirt road that led up to the mansion where Luther resided. A light breeze had begun to kick-up, and the unseasonably cold air wreaked havoc with his knees. Four years of college football had seen to it that Justus would have something to remember his playing days by, and three operations later, his knees still had the unwelcome ability to grab his attention.

He reached viewing distance of the house and quickly slipped behind a bush when he saw that someone was outside. Underneath the front door light, he could distinctly see his target, apparently enjoying a cigarette in the cool air.

Justus pulled a picture from his pocket, provided to him by Lord Innon. The photo depicted Luther, looking queerly like a priest saying Mass, taken only a few months earlier. He easily confirmed the identity of his prey and slowly crept closer, remaining in the shadows behind the foliage.

As Luther turned to walk back into his house, Justus sprang upon him from behind. The eighteen inches of chain sunk deep into the skin around his victim's neck. Justus' arms flexed, and his heart rate increased as the excitement of the kill sent adrenaline shooting through his veins. As was his custom, Justus would choke his victim until he was within seconds of death, then quickly release the tension. When he was confident brain activity was at a minimum, he would look into the bewildered eyes of his prey before snapping his neck, permanently turning off the lights of yet another piece of scum.

Luther felt the chain-link sink into his neck, cutting off the flow of oxygen to his lungs. He closed his eyes, forcing himself to meditate—to focus.

After two minutes or so of struggling, the body went limp in Justus' arms. He loosened his grip after another few seconds had passed by, bringing his victim to his desired brink of full, clinical death, yet not quite stepping over the line.

He slid his arms under the armpits of his victim, moving him into the light of the foyer. Justus let the body fall face first on the ground as he used his other hand to close the front door. He heard the familiar crunching sound of a nose shattering.

He stood above the body, chuckling to himself at the ease of the hit. The body still showed some minimal signs of life, though he didn't imagine that this brain held a concept of reality any longer.

So let's take a look at the man who so terrified those other two pansy-ass pagans!

He reached down and grabbed the left arm of his victim, rolling the body over in one easy motion so that it was face up.

Justus gasped, his hand quickly rising to his mouth to prevent an uncharacteristic scream. He bit down hard, drawing blood. His eyes remained fixated on the face of his victim. To his dismay, it was not the face of the notorious Luther, his intended target. The eyes that looked up at him, lost in a brain-damaged void, were unmistakably familiar.

It was Lord Aaoth.

Justus turned his head away and did something that he had not done in his entire adult life without the aid of alcohol. He vomited.

He was still experiencing dry heaves when, out of the darkness in the next room, someone cleared his throat.

ii

"After all these years, you're finally talking some sense, Vannie," Yerik Nesterov stated with an obvious feeling of satisfaction.

The two once again sat in the diner outside of the town of Ephesus, where the initial futility of their situation had fallen hard upon them years ago. Yet today, the atmosphere was different. A sense of urgency pushed them past their feelings of impotence.

"Can the lectures, little brother," Vanya retorted. "I don't think we have much time. I need things set up so that I can make one call and be out of here with the boys within fifteen minutes."

"That's not a problem, Vannie," Yerik added confidently. "We can have a dozen men within striking distance at all times from here out, and I'll set up a toll-free number so you can give us the signal without even having to speak. Just dial the number, we'll trace the call and have our men there in full force in less than ten minutes."

"We'll also need new identities. I'll want immediate plastic surgery for myself."

Yerik shook his head. "Papa's not going to want anybody messing with that pretty face Vannie, you'll be fine with—"

"I'm not taking any chances, Yerik. Luther's people are everywhere, and Jeffrey won't rest until he's found his son."

"Oh yes he will," Yerik muttered under his breath.

"What was that?" Vanya stopped herself long enough to try to hear her brother's comment.

"Nothing, Vannie, just talking to myself. Listen, you leave the details to me. We'll get Papa's best guys on it, and I will be within an hour's trip of you at all times. Just do not leave the boys alone, and give us a call when you're ready."

"How will I get the number?" Vanya inquired, not fully comfortable with leaving all the details to someone else.

"In two days you will receive some junk mail, one of those million-dollar sweepstakes things. The toll-free number will be in there, along with any other pertinent information. Justus should be getting back from his vacation out West in the next day or so, and I'll have him post a man on you at all times. You will never be out of our sight."

A moment passed as the two stared at each other.

"And what about the device you think is imbedded in Jesse?" Yerik inquired soberly.

Vanya sighed deeply. "I don't know, Yerik. Whether manmade or not, I am going to have to trust God on this one."

A slight smile emerged on Yerik's face. "You're a true believer, sis. Still, practical Yerik will see what else he can find out."

"Thank you," Vanya spoke with sincere gratitude. "How's Papa doing?"

"It was a rough go of it for a while, but I'd say much better. He spent ten days in jail after he discharged a firearm—something he's not supposed to have in the first place. But it looks like the judge is about to accept an injunction to prevent the feds from doing any further surveillance. The case against him is crumbling, though we still haven't found the mole. I need to tell you though, Vannie, once he's free and clear, he may not wait for your signal to come down and get you and the boys."

"He has to, Yerik," Vanya pleaded. "If he doesn't listen to me on this one, something very bad is going to happen."

Yerik looked at his sister with a concerned expression. "These people really have you shaken up, huh?" He wasn't used to seeing this side of her.

Vanya tried to give a casual look around the diner. "You have no idea."

He hesitated, then tried to feign a smile. "Don't worry, sis. Everything will work out fine."

You're a poor liar, my dear brother, Vanya thought.

Her stomach was tensing up, as it had been doing constantly since her dream. The moment she had been waiting for over the past six years was now upon her, and she did not want to take a single misstep. Vanya had resolved within herself that if it was God's will that she not make it, so be it. But she prayed that no harm would come to the boys.

However, she could not deny the feeling of dread, sensing that she was to be put to the test in this flight, and she was afraid—more so than she had ever been in her life. This was more than just a simple escape from a raving lunatic. This was the beginning of something—something almost supernatural—that would probably not end during the twin's natural lives.

She could only pray that her faith would be strong enough. But for now, she would settle for her hands to stop shaking.

iii

"Well, you've got me on this one, Father." Dr. Luke Hilgers was truly perplexed.

Father Daniel looked up from his hospital bed, his head still pounding, though much less so today. Dr. Hilgers motioned to the three MRI scans on the wall.

The good doctor continued. "Here is your scan when you first came in two months ago; a massive—if not unusual—hemorrhage that passed from one side of your brain to the other. I would say your chances of surviving at that point were about nil."

He pointed then to the second scan. "This was taken the next week. It's amazing, but it seems like the hemorrhage is beginning the process of resolving itself here. I'd like to say it was because I am a great physician, but the truth is I didn't operate—I wouldn't have even known where to begin."

SEED

Dr. Hilgers looked back at Father Daniel as if about to unveil the prestige. "And here is today. We ran this one right after you regained consciousness this morning, and your brain scan looks completely normal."

Father Daniel managed a slight grin that somewhat betrayed the depth of the gratitude he felt. "It would seem that a slow cure is a sure cure. So what is it you're telling me, Doctor?"

"I'm saying that, if I were not already a believer, I'd be one now."

17

PR: So Madame Opfree, could you please explain to our
     listening audience what you mean when you say 'this
     is the final generation'?

MO: The old way is ending, and a new era is about to
     begin.

PR: And what do you mean by 'the old way'?

MO: A new age is upon us, and man's archaic beliefs in
     an omnipotent god will finally cease. All this will
     come to pass before this generation perishes.

PR: And why do you believe this to be true, Madame
     Opfree?

MO: It is not what I believe. It has been written in the
     stars.

– Excerpts from *The Phil Rivers Show*

i

Lord Innon lay on top of his bed at the Cavalier Hotel, finishing what was left of his room service meal. He had been flipping through the channels, trying to find something that would catch his interest, but to no avail.

He followed his last bite of lamb chop with a few gulps of wine, then put his tray aside. His stomach did not feel too good. He had been waiting for the call from Justus stating that "it" had been done. Then he would catch the first plane to Toronto, needing to attend to some "regional business" (his oversight of the entire North American region for the Brotherhood never permitted the possibility of boredom), then back to Sardis for what he hoped to be the final meeting of the Conclave.

Innon jumped as the phone rang.

SEED

Ease up, good man, this is the good news you've been waiting for!

Before he allowed his moment of anxiety to enwrap him any further, he yanked the phone from his receiver.

"Justus?"

The voice on the other end sounded annoyed.

"I told you not to use my name on the phone, jack-ass!"

It was Justus. A feeling of relief swept through Innon's being.

"Is…is it done?"

"Oh, it's done all right. It's damned *well* done! You need to get your pagan-ass out here now!"

Innon was puzzled. Was something wrong?

"Why…why do you need me to come out there?" he questioned.

"Listen, bitch! Don't get squeamish on me now. We had an agreement, and I'm ready to close the deal with you. Things didn't go quite as planned, but I guess you can say you got a two-for-one deal. You hearing me, *my lord?*"

The manner in which Justus said "my lord" contained so much sarcasm and contempt in its tone that Innon had to hold back an instinctive fury within him. He had grown weary of this Catholic fool's insults.

"I still don't see why I need to—"

"Listen, you piece of shit, I'd hate to have to come looking for you, if you know what I mean! Get your satanic-ass out here within the next half-hour, or you'll no longer have to worry how many shopping days there are until Christmas!"

Innon heard a click, followed by the dial tone. Why the hell did Justus want him down at Luther's place? That was plain stupid. And what did he mean by, "two-for-one"?

Innon was flustered, to say the least, but there was one thing he was sure of now. He did not want the nation's most infamous hit man coming after him. He threw on his overcoat and quickly slid out the door.

Being well past midnight, there were few people out driving. In fact, by the time Innon reached Luther's place, he had spotted no more than a dozen cars out on the road. When he came upon a rental car parked perhaps a quarter-mile from the residence, Innon pulled over. He was pretty certain that it must belong to Justus.

This is pretty stupid, he thought. *Coming to the scene of the crime.*

Innon was about to step out of the car when suddenly the car stereo turned on at an earsplitting volume. He scrambled to shut off the system as the oldie song *I'm a believer* blared across the speakers. He slammed the knobs on the system, and it stopped as suddenly as it had begun; yet his ears were still ringing.

He did his best to recompose himself, then exited the vehicle once again and began to walk.

Innon did take some solace in the fact that this was old-hat for Justus, and that he must know what he was doing. As he approached the house, Innon saw Justus' silhouette standing in the doorway. Justus beckoned for Innon to hurry up, then returned inside himself.

Innon quickened his pace, wanting to get this over with. He entered through the front door, then closed it behind him.

You idiot! Fingerprints! he thought, too late.

Innon pulled a handkerchief out of his pocket and wiped the inside of the knob. He turned around to see a body lying on the floor covered with what used to be a white sheet. It was well stained with blood now.

"I'm waiting, *my lord.*"

There was that sarcastic tone again. Innon could see the light coming from the next room. He took one last look at the covered body and entered the study, where he could smell the stench of Justus' cigar.

He gasped as he entered the room. Justus' back was to him, continuing to puff away at his cigar while obviously intrigued with Luther's library collection. But what made his spine tingle was sitting in the chair to his immediate right.

It was Lord Aaoth.

Only something was wrong. Aaoth did not look at him with eyes of recognition, and as Innon moved closer he could see that the man was drooling.

"My God," Innon gasped, with his eyes still fixed on Aaoth.

"Interesting choice of words," Justus replied from his right.

But actually, what he heard was not Justus' voice at all, yet it was still familiar. It was...it was...

"Lord Innon. So good of you to come to my home. But you know, we really should not be meeting like this."

Luther!

Innon spun around, now terrified beyond words.

"What... what have you done to him?" he managed to get out.

"Me? Nothing actually. That Catholic you sent here to visit me just didn't seem to be all that bright. But then again, that's a Catholic for you. Always playing on the losing team. It seems curious to me, Lord Innon, that you decided to join that team. As far as Lord Aaoth goes, it would be safe to say that he is pretty clearly a vegetable now. It's kind of ironic in a way, isn't it? A fruit pairing up with a vegetable?" Luther chuckled to himself.

Innon could not move. At this juncture, despite his best attempts to present the contrary, he was frozen in fear.

"Here, Innon," Luther continued. "I want to show you how I just saved you a lot of money."

Luther walked over to the body on the floor and pulled off the bloodstained sheet. Innon gagged at what he saw.

It did not necessarily surprise him to see the remains of Bartholomew Justus on the floor. His body was covered with small dime-shaped burns. Yet what drew Innon to a state of nausea was seeing Justus' bloody innards protruding from his mouth. A look of terror had solidified on the corpse's face.

"He probably would have killed me too, Innon, *but I do not believe he had the stomach for it!*" Luther laughed out loud this time.

Lord Innon closed his eyes, took a deep breath, and resigned himself to whatever was going to happen next.

"What are you going to do to me?" he breathed, now with surprising calmness in his voice.

"Ah, always to the point, yes, Lord Innon? Well I have had a lot of time to think about this, and we have one little problem to discuss. Though Lord Aaoth is permanently, shall we say, *disposed* at this time, he asked me to relay to the members of the Conclave his decision to change his vote."

"You son of a bitch," Innon retorted, the tension beginning to re-enter his voice.

"You will get no argument from me on that one, my lord. Anyhow, that seems to leave us with the issue of one last, little, insignificant vote."

"I told you," Innon attempted to add emphasis. "You will never get my vote."

Luther smiled and moved over to his chair behind a large oak desk. He sat down, spun himself around in the chair twice, then put his hands behind his head and his feet up on his desk.

"Have you ever heard of the rock opera called *Tommy*?" Luther inquired.

"The what?" Innon responded, not understanding what this had to do with anything.

"No, Innon, actually it was 'The *Who*'. But that was a good guess. You see, it was about this little boy, Tommy, who experiences something so traumatic in his childhood that he ends up deaf, dumb, and blind."

Innon was thoroughly confused.

"What are you getting at, Luther?"

Luther didn't immediately answer. He smiled, got up from his seat, and walked over towards Innon. By this time, Lord Innon was plastered against the wall. Luther moved his face to within three inches of Innon's.

"It really is amazing, my lord, the power of belief. Would you like to experience something... *traumatic*?"

ii

Vanya walked with Jesse and Tobias to the final resting place of their mother. Through the years, she had greatly desired to come here, but she knew that coming on her own could potentially raise suspicion; and it had taken her this long to garner the courage to bring Jesse. Yet, all things considered, and the reality of their imminent flight, Vanya recognized this would be perhaps her last chance to visit Marisha.

She had painstakingly measured out the exact distance from their home to the point where Jesse had first experienced the trouble breathing years back, and she was not surprised to find that it was almost exactly a mile. The distance to Jeffrey's previous residence, the land on which Marisha's grave rested, was a little more than a half-mile. According to Jeffrey, the walk through the woods to their mother's location was no more than another quarter-mile.

When Vanya had first posed the idea to Jeffrey, she was quite confused by his initial response. He stared at her with a glazed-over look, then his eyes started to fill, and he quickly looked away. He took a moment, she supposed mulling over distances, and responded coolly, "Sure, whatever."

"Wow! What a cool house!" Tobias called out as they reached the end of the driveway to the home in which their mother had lived. Despite the fact that there was nothing in particular that would make the place seem creepy, Vanya still felt a chill go down her back as she reflected on the events which had taken place there.

"Are we going inside, Nanny Vanya?" Jesse inquired.

Vanya shook her head. "No, Jesse. We are looking for a path through the woods here." Then, with an attempt not to produce any anxiety, she said, "How are you feeling, Jes."

"I feel great!"

The boys ran off in the direction Vanya had been told to look for the path. It was only a few minutes before they squealed in delight upon finding it.

Vanya stayed close to Jesse's side as they emerged from the wooded path into the clearing. Her familiarity with the area returned as she again had to fight away feelings of absence still deep within her.

As if drawn by some unseen force, Jesse and Tobias ran straight towards the grassy knoll where the small headstone rested, which itself barely emerged from the ground. Upon reaching it, they stood in silence, looking down. Vanya arrived a moment later, still closely monitoring Jesse.

"This is it, Nanny Vanya?" Tobias whispered.

"Yes," Vanya responded, speaking barely louder than a whisper herself as she felt her voice quiver.

They stood there for a moment in silence, then Jesse suddenly looked up—almost as if he had heard something.

"What is it, Jesse? Are you feeling okay?" Vanya inquired, her heart rate suddenly jumping.

But he did not respond. His eyes fixed upon a small tree, perhaps ten feet tall, only a few steps from his mother's grave. He slowly walked up to it, as if in a dream state, then placed his hand upon it.

Tobias also watched with curiosity as his brother seemed to caress the small trunk, his lips moving but no sound emerging. Vanya moved closer to Jesse, then got down on one knee in front of him.

"Jesse, what is it?"

He slowly turned his gaze to her, seemingly lost in a reverie.

"Can we come here again, Nanny Vanya? This is a good place."

Vanya did not know exactly how to respond. She thought she heard a faint sound—not unlike wind chimes—but then it was gone. With that, Jesse turned and looked out towards the eastern sky. They were perhaps an hour from twilight, and you could already see the moon rising; it would be a full moon that night. Jesse's expression transformed to one of profound sadness.

"It's... it's good for us to be here."

iii

"Dr. Sanger, I presume?"

Yerik Nesterov had just entered the darkened room where the thoroughly beaten Dr. Sanger had been brought before him by two of his father's henchmen.

"Who are you?" Sanger spoke, spitting blood through the newly acquired gaps in his teeth.

"I am a concerned citizen, you might say. And I have a few questions to ask you, questions regarding a certain Jesse Chardin."

Sanger's eyes widened—as much as swollen eyes could—and he looked up to Yerik.

"Whatever interest you have in that boy," he spoke with strange conviction in his voice, considering his predicament, "I would advise you to walk away."

Yerik smiled. "Well, it's not my habit to ignore sound medical advice, but I just want to know the nature of the device which you or your friends planted in this boy's body, and how we disable it."

Sanger stiffened as he tried to move his arms, which were beginning to cramp up, being tied tightly behind his back. "Device? What are you talking about?"

A backhand sailed swiftly and firmly across Sanger's face. He cried out, then released a slow groan.

This interrogation thing was not Yerik's forte—he felt a bit cliché in his approach. Nor did the fact that some of his father's men were observing how he handled this situation escape him. Yet time was running short; even he could sense a foreboding imminence of... of *something*... just over the horizon.

"I am talking about whatever you put in him that makes him sick and stop breathing when he leaves a certain radius from his house."

Sanger looked up again, and the expression of confusion began to fade from his countenance. "You look familiar, do I know you?"

Yerik ignored the comment and placed his right hand around Sanger's neck. "Tell me about the implant!"

Sanger spoke steadily. "There is no implant. What you speak of has no natural cause. It is the Counselor, Luther. It is a supernatural web of unknown origin. And it is not just the Chardin boy, it is all of us."

"You are talking fairy tales, man!"

Sanger shook his head, his breathing now slowed. "I see that you are not a believer. But we are all animals in a cage here. We've made our choice. I advise you to walk away."

Yerik was becoming more unsettled. He looked at the other two men in the room, who were just itching to finish the job on this pathetic man, but he could even see a sense of curiosity with a splash of fear in their eyes as well. Still, Yerik needed more answers.

"Whatever you believe it to be, Doctor, I need to know how to override it."

The doctor, despite his predicament, began to chuckle. "You're not listening to me, but either way, the answer to your question is quite simple. If some force holds the boy here, then only a greater force can overcome it. Simple logic, but you can trust me on this one, you will not find a greater force."

18

"I am the Lizard King
I can do anything"

– Jim Morrison
Not to Touch the Earth

i

Luther sat at the far end of the five-sided table gently smiling to himself as Lord Galethog stood to officially announce what everyone in the room already knew.

"After seventy-five cycles, our Conclave has come to its consummation; a successor to our Highest of High Priests has been chosen." Galethog looked towards Luther. "Father Luther, would you please stand?"

Luther nodded and rose from his seat. He appeared taller in stature than any of the other Council members had remembered. He maintained a regal air about him as Galethog continued to speak.

"You have been elected, through a unanimous decision by the four active Arch-Ministers of the Church, the Brotherhood of the Coming Prince, to serve in the capacity of the Grand Elder, the Highest of High Priests. Do you accept this honor?"

"I do," replied Luther in a manner which for some unascertainable reason sent shivers down Galethog's spine.

"Very well," Galethog replied, quickly shaking off the chill. "Then, as has been written, we must hold an ordination ceremony within the next three cycles to consecrate this most sacred event."

Luther nodded and then spoke. "Lord, if I may, I offer my own Temple as the site for the ordination ceremony, to be held three cycles hence. In addition, I propose to consecrate this most sacred occasion with the ancient rites of our forefathers."

Lord Galaas looked at Luther somewhat puzzled. "You wish to be ordained with the blood of an innocent?"

Luther again nodded. "Yes, my brother. I do."

Galethog broke in. "Very well, I feel it would be more than appropriate to consecrate the ceremony with the sacrifice of a goat, and if no one else has any objections, I—"

"No, Lord Galethog," Luther interrupted. "The blood of an innocent *child*."

Several gasps erupted from the chambers. Luther was aware of the fact that human sacrifice in the Church's practice had long been abolished as the Brotherhood had attempted to become more appealing to the mainstream.

"Surely, Father Luther, you realize—"

"I realize that we have become a flock of weaklings and cowards, afraid to profess our true beliefs and practice our true rituals. We have become political, instead of spiritual, animals—a body filled with the rotting stench of non-believers."

The remaining members of the Supreme Council sat in amazement as Luther continued on. "This behavior, this fear of expressing one's true beliefs has caused the ongoing erosion of the Christian Church, and we do not seem to be interested in learning from the mistakes of our nemesis."

Luther felt the power surge within him as he persisted. "We will become strong again, one undivided Church under *He Who Has No Origin*. Shedding the blood of an innocent will mark that new direction, the new covenant, a return to our old but true ways."

There was an endless silence. Finally, a Council member spoke.

"And how," added Lord Thaaoth, somewhat uncomfortably, "do you propose we select this innocent child?"

"He has already been chosen by the Master."

Lord Galaas' previous look of surprise slowly turned into one of intrigue. "And who, then, is the Chosen One?"

Luther slowly gazed at each member of the Council sitting before him, sensing now a feeling of guarded excitement. They would follow him. Their hearts were the Master's.

DOMINION

"That is my concern, and the concern of my *Father's*, not yours."

ii

Vanya sat with Jesse at the harpsichord playing the music he so loved. It had been nearly a week since he had awakened crying, the morning following their visit to Marisha's grave, and not for the first time there had been blood on his sheets. These crying spells seemed to run like clockwork, and if she didn't know better, she would have thought the boy had a menstrual cycle.

As usual, the best remedy for Jesse was the harpsichord. After a day or so he would stop crying and just sit with a blank stare on his face. Usually, by the time seventy-two hours had passed (along with all the strength in Vanya's fingers) Jesse would be back to his old self. She was afraid to admit to herself, however, that these "spells" were getting longer and more intense.

Jesse continued to sit and stare as Vanya played on. Tobias would periodically come up and rub his brother's back, trying to get him to snap out of the trance so they could go play. He had also become accustomed to these spells and worked hard to help Jesse out of them. When they seemed to last longer than usual, he and his Nanny Vanya would hold Jesse's hands and pray for him.

Seated at the harpsichord, watching the zombie of a child sitting next to her, Vanya prayed silently.

Dear God, she began, *I've been patient these years. I have followed Your will without concern for myself. But I cannot let this go on. This is more than the boys can take, especially Jesse. If I do not receive clarity as to Your will by next week, I am leaving with the boys. I cannot stand by and let this continue. I made a promise to my sister. I promised I'd protect her babies, and that's what I intend to do.*

Vanya shivered. She knew it was wrong to give God an ultimatum. But she was not asking for herself, this was for her nephews.

She was resolved to the fact that God would maintain His mysterious silence. As she moved toward the completion of her prayer, Vanya nearly jumped out of her seat when she felt Jesse's hand placed on top of hers. She looked down to see his bright blue eyes smiling up at her.

"*Do not fear, Vanya,*" he spoke in a somewhat dreamy voice. "*For all is unfolding as my Father has planned.*"

Vanya gasped, and then blinked her eyes. She looked to Jesse again and saw him sitting there with the same blank stare as before.

Did that just happen? she asked herself, but quickly, and with a somewhat terrified realization, she slipped into her next thought.

And exactly who does he mean, when he says, 'Father?'

iii

"He is what?" Alexandre Nesterov was doing all he could to restrain himself.

"He is dead, sir."

Mikhail Ostankino did not enjoy being the bearer of bad news. As he puffed away, somewhat nervously, at his filterless cigarette, he reflected on the horror stories about the plight of "the messenger" in Mafia families. Yeah, they were all Russians, but they'd seen *The Godfather,* hadn't they? He swallowed hard, trying to conceal his anxiety.

"How did this happen?" Nesterov pursued.

Ostankino took in another puff, then cleared his throat. "He was found at St. Origen Catholic Church in a town in Tennessee called Sardis. He was left on top of the altar."

Alexandre Nesterov had a disgusted look on his face. "And?"

"Well, sir," Ostankino continued. "It seems that his... his innards were cut out and...ah...placed in his mouth."

Nesterov did not break his gaze from Ostankino's eyes, though Ostankino did not meet his stare for more than a few seconds at a time.

"So he bled to death?"

"Not exactly, sir."

"Can you relieve me of this suspense, Mikhail?" Nesterov was growing wearisome of this game.

"Well, sir, according to the coroner, his heart just stopped."

Nesterov shook his head and sat back in his chair. "*Blei!* This is the last thing I need right now."

Nesterov got up from his chair and walked to the window overlooking the city. It was only his second day off of house arrest and full surveillance. He looked out over his organization's far-reaching territory, wondering what was happening to his daughter and grandchildren.

Still with his back to him, Nesterov addressed the arrogant, at times spineless, yet still loyal Ostankino. "Was there anything else significant regarding the death of Mr. Justus, Mikhail?"

This time Ostankino drew in a much longer hit from his nearly completed cigarette. He exhaled slowly, clearly a bit unnerved by some thought. "Actually, sir," he began, "there was. He had a...a pentagram carved into his chest."

Nesterov turned and stared long and hard at his underling. He had never in his life come across the occult, but now he had two separate incidences in a short period of time. Could they be related? Or was it just that the activities of the occult were more prevalent than he had believed?

Either way, he had an uneasy feeling. Vanya was right. This was no minor operation. This was bigger than the both of them could have possibly imagined. If the occult was that widespread, how could even he expect to protect his daughter and grandchildren? Even so, Nesterov knew one thing. He had to get them out of there, and out now, before this got beyond what even the notorious Alexandre Nesterov could handle.

What in God's name is going on?

Ostankino smothered the last bit of his cigarette in his hand, tossed it in the trash and began reaching inside his coat pocket for another.

Nesterov, his voice a bit more even, shook his head. "That is a nasty habit, Mikhail, those things, they will kill you."

Mikhail shrugged as he lit his new cigarette. "We are all going to die... someday."

iv

Pietro Cardinal Colomba sat in the small room in the Sistine Chapel. It had been nearly a month-long papal conclave, but he now held the title, "Holy Father."

He had thought carrying that title would be the culmination of a lifelong dream. But instead of unbridled joy, he was experiencing an internal battle which was of unknown origin. The reign of Leo XIV, a man Pietro himself had helped ascend to power, had begun to open his eyes to much that Pietro had previously not allowed himself to see. His appointment to Secretary of State kept him close to his native Rome, but also exploited a deepening chasm within him between what Pietro had believed to be truth and what he was having a more and more difficult time denying.

No doubt the other cardinals had elected him believing that he would continue in the footsteps of his predecessor, Leo. Yet Pietro was filled with more confusion now than he had ever been. As he struggled to sort things out in his head, from behind him, he heard a familiar voice.

"Peter."

The accent was slight, but unmistakably Russian.

Pietro turned around to see three men standing before him. In between a stately appearing man and a filthy vagabond stood his would-be predecessor, Christopher.

"Christopher... my God... how did..." and suddenly a wave of anxiety swept over Pietro, followed by an unexpected sense of resolution. "Are you here… have you come to kill me?"

Christopher slowly shook his head. "No, Peter, I have not."

Pietro looked anxiously to each of the other two men, who remained silent.

He cleared his throat, feeling the anxiety battle against the resolve. "I am certain, though, that you are not unaware that I was one of the primary men behind the act to have you removed from office."

Christopher nodded. "Yes, Peter, I am."

"And you would know better than anyone that the charges were fabrications. Yet I still pursued them, conspiring with others that were against you. I had believed, at least at the time, that it was what was best for the Church."

Christopher again nodded and allowed a moment to pass before speaking again. "Peter, it is a sad statement that many leaders within the Bride have conspired against the Truth at some time or another, supposedly for the good of the Church. Though, the truth be known, we must persevere *always* in the Light, as the darkness must be given no quarter."

Pietro stared at Christopher in silent acknowledgement as Christopher continued.

"This all had to come to pass. What men have intended for evil, God has used for good. I have not come to condemn or expose you, but to give you a gift. A gift that was given to me in this very edifice, not by man, but by the Holy Spirit. And today, of my own volition, I will relinquish it unto you."

With that, the two other men exited the room.

Pietro looked to Christopher, the realization of what was transpiring overwhelming him as a tear escaped from his eyelid. "I believe I understand. Holy Father, Christopher, will you hear my confession?"

19

"And it was then that I witnessed the voice for the light returning to the flesh, in the form of song. Yet with this song was carried a counter-melody, which hid itself from the light for a time and a time and a half."

– St. Vincent of the Sand (967-996)

i

Tobias was having a difficult time sleeping. He had heard his father return to their home in the late evening, drawing him out of his dream. Then someone else had come. Tobias could hear the two men moving around and speaking, but he could not fully discern their conversation.

Allowing his curiosity to get the best of him, he crawled out of bed and slowly crept down the stairs. Knowing his father would not be pleased seeing him up and awake, Tobias sat on the third step from the bottom, straining to listen to the conversation in the next room.

"Yes, Jesse *always* sleeps in the walk-in closet. I don't allow him to sleep anywhere else." It was his father's voice.

Then the other man spoke. "I will instruct the servants as to his whereabouts. It will be one week from tonight. You must leave the front door unlocked. They will retrieve the boy an hour before midnight."

His father spoke again. "Why not just let me bring him over then?"

"No," the other interrupted. "I will need you to coordinate the preparations for the ceremony with the Arch-Ministers."

"That would be an honor, Father. What exactly do you have planned for Jesse?"

There was a long pause, then the other man again spoke. "At the midnight hour, I will plunge the sacred blade through his heart and be christened with his blood. I will then assume the position of Grand Elder, the Highest of High Priests, the next in a sequence of steps towards my final destiny."

There was another, much longer pause, accompanied by some moving around. Tobias sat, frozen in fear. Could they really be talking about killing his brother? Again, it was the other man who spoke.

"Is there something *wrong*, Jeffrey?"

"I...I—" Even Tobias could recognize that his father's voice was quivering.

"Go on, Jeffrey, say what you must." the other's tone was full of contempt.

Jeffrey tried, unsuccessfully, to compose himself. "I don't know, it's just that... well, as much as I detest the sight of Jesse, I still feel that he is a part of Marisha. As strange as it may seem, I've gotten used to having him around, and despite my efforts, I know my son has grown pretty close to him."

"Your weakness is repulsive, Jeffrey," the voice stated in an even, yet still clearly disgusted tone. "Perhaps I have chosen the wrong man to serve as caretaker for my son."

"No, Father, I don't mean that, I—" Jeffrey stopped dead in mid-sentence, fully digesting what Luther had just said. "Your what?"

"That is right, Jeffrey," the second voice stated in a condescending tone. "*My* son. *My* seed. The product of my and Marisha's... *understanding*."

Silence.

"And I would say more, Jeffrey. Despite your sharing a 'biological' connection with the other boy, it has been revealed to me that he too will share in my spirit—as a son to a father."

Tobias heard more pacing from the room.

"Yes, Jeffrey, *feel* the power that accompanies your anger now, and use that strength to destroy these feelings of weakness. This is the will of the Great Seraph, which has been foretold to me. Do not allow your petty fears to prevent us from receiving that which is rightfully ours."

After a brief pause, a tense, shaky voice replied, "I will obey the will of the Master."

Tobias had already heard more than he could handle. He stood up from his sitting place and reached for the banister to steady himself. His heart froze as the banister's weak supports let out a seemingly deafening *creeeeeeeeeeak*.

"What was that?" he heard the second voice inquire.

"I'm not sure," his father replied, now hastening towards the staircase.

Tobias stood petrified, not able to move. He might be able to make it to the top of the stairs, but his father would most likely see or hear him before he made it to his room. Then he would know he had been listening. As the footsteps grew closer, Tobias did the only thing he felt he could. He turned around and began to walk down the remaining stairs.

His father arrived seconds later, followed by a man he recognized as Luther, his father's boss.

"Tobias, what are you doing up so late?" his father inquired.

Luther stared at Tobias with suspicion. Tobias did not look up to meet his gaze. He quickly remembered what Vanya had told him to do when he was frightened.

The Lord is my shepherd, I shall not...

"Tobias, I'm speaking to you!" Jeffrey demanded.

Tobias looked up this time and now saw a puzzled look on Luther's face. He had to think of something to say quickly.

"I...I heard you down here, and I thought maybe you would read me a bedtime story."

It was a poor lie, but it seemed to do the trick. His father sighed. "For the love of the Devil, Tobias, it's two o'clock in the morning! Get back up to bed, and I'll be up in a few minutes to tuck you in. Got it?"

"Yes, Daddy," Tobias replied, quickly turning and heading up the stairs. As he reached the top, he looked back down to find Luther still staring at him with the same puzzled look on his face.

Tobias shot into his bedroom, hopped into his bed and buried his face in his pillow, finally allowing himself to cry. By the time Jeffrey came to his room a half-hour later, it appeared that Tobias was asleep.

He was not. In fact, Tobias wondered seriously if he would ever be able to sleep again.

DOMINION

ii

Silence.

It was a vow which had been held by the Twelve Carmelite Brothers for forty years. In their modest monastery high amongst the Ural Mountains, they had dedicated themselves to a life of simplicity and prayer, completely isolated from the outside world.

However, today would be different. A nod from Brother Eli had awakened a sense of anticipation among the brothers. They gathered in the main hall, kneeling in a circle, leaving only enough space for their superior to join and bring the circle to completion.

The brothers exchanged anxious glances. Their beards had grown long and gray, as most were reaching their late sixties and early seventies.

A robed figure entered the room, kneeling in the opening left in the circle. He spread his arms, palms out, then reached up to remove the hood from his head.

But as their superior knelt and removed his hood, it was evident that he did not share their long, gray beards. Nor did his skin bear the heavy sags and wrinkles which inevitably accompanied old age. It was, as the remaining brothers would attest, a miracle that they had grown to accept. Brother Eli had not aged a day in the forty-some years they had known him.

With his arms still spread, Brother Eli shattered the forty-year vow with a brief phrase; three words, for which the remaining brothers had waited over four decades, rang out throughout the halls.

"It is time..."

iii

"Pray and fast..."

These were the words Father Daniel had unmistakably heard during his prayer in front of the Blessed Sacrament. This would be his third day of consuming nothing but water and the consecrated bread and wine for each daily Mass.

SEED

He was not exactly sure for whom or for what he was sacrificing, only that he had a sense that there was a spiritual stronghold of a dark origin that must be brought down. The ramifications for failing in this call, Father Daniel sensed, would be dire for many multitudes of souls.

Still, he did not sense that some great good would be the result of this period of prayer and fasting, but only a slight mitigation, even delay, of some great evil.

"I am Your instrument, Lord. Use me as You will."

20

Allied Press ~

MOSCOW - Known as "The Bloodless Coup of Russia", the transition of the governing body of one of the most powerful regimes in the history of the world has now come to full fruition with the installation of Nikolai Petrov as premier.

In his first act as premier, Petrov asked forgiveness from the world for the "horrific acts against humanity" by Russia and the Soviet Union throughout history, as well as the many "errors which we ourselves have spread throughout the world, especially in the last century."

The "Coup" was led by the Eastern Catholic Patriarch, Cardinal Yuri Bogdanov, who was by Petrov's side for the installation. He has called on all Russians to enter into a six-year period of penance for the past "sins against the true heart of the motherland", with the seventh year to be declared a year of "Jubilee".

In a world that has witnessed a steady decline in traditional religion, the past three years have seen a major resurgence in Russian participation in both the Orthodox and Catholic faiths. A dramatic drop in crime has also accompanied the increased interest in traditionalism, though sociologists do not acknowledge any correlation between the two phenomena.

SEED

i

Tobias snuck out of his bed after he heard the front door close behind his father. He had spent the entire week following his eavesdropping episode in bed, not feeling the strength to get out. Nanny Vanya had implored him to tell her what was wrong, but he was unable to. It was as if he could not bear to bring the words to his lips. So he remained silent.

The sun had set again on another day. This was a night that Tobias prayed would never arrive. He slowly sat up amongst his sheets, and with a deepening sense of gloom, he got out of bed. Still, despite all the feelings that were welling within him, he was resolved in what he must do. It was as if there was something in his mind, in some hidden recess of ancient knowledge, compelling him, assuring Tobias that it was for this reason that he was born.

Moving slowly down the hall, careful not to wake Nanny Vanya, Tobias placed his right hand on the doorknob to Jesse's room. He opened the door to find his brother fast asleep. Tobias let out a deep sigh, then moved into the closet-made-room.

He stood over Jesse, looking at how still he lay. A momentary rush of panic gripped Tobias.

He's already dead!

However, almost as if to quell his fear, Jesse let out a light, sleepy moan. Tobias felt his heartbeat return to normal. He reached down and gently shook his brother's arm.

"Jes?"

His brother let out another light moan and shifted his position. Tobias had to be careful to only lightly awaken him, for he did not feel Jesse would follow through with his instructions if he had all his wits about him.

He shook Jesse again, whispering, "Jes?"

"Wha?" was Jesse's response, still without opening his eyes.

"Shhhh," Tobias said, soothingly. "You've got to get up for a minute. I've got a surprise for you in my bed."

Jesse did not respond immediately.

"Daddy will k-kill me."

"No, he won't," Tobias urged. "He's gone. And it will only take a sec."

Though not responding verbally, Jesse rolled around and sat up, eyes still closed.

"Okay, Jes, keep your eyes closed and let me hold your arm. I'll take care of you, brother."

"Thanks, Toby," Jesse responded, allowing Tobias to help him to his feet.

Tobias opened the door and looked both ways down the hall. No sign of Nanny Vanya. He moved quietly down the hall, guiding his half-awake brother with his right hand. It seemed like ages had passed by the time they reached Tobias' room.

As they moved towards his bed, Tobias thought he heard a floorboard creak in the hallway. He waited a tense few seconds, feeling his heart speed up, but he did not hear another sound.

You're just a big chicken, Toby, making up sounds in your head! he thought.

Yet his heartbeat continued to accelerate. Tobias moved Jesse in position to get into the bed.

"Okay, Jesse," he whispered. "Now lie back."

Jesse did as his brother instructed without even a murmur. He even snuggled up to the pillow as Tobias pulled his covers over him. Tobias then stood back from the bed, looking from his peacefully sleeping brother, to the door, and then back. He began to feel tears welling up in his eyes, but he made a conscious effort to stop himself immediately. Once again, he took a deep breath and moved out of his room.

Back in the hallway, Tobias kept his eyes to the floor as he moved down the hall. His heart was thumping so loudly in his mind that he barely heard the second creak.

Tobias stopped dead in his tracks. He looked up to see Nanny Vanya, in her nightgown, standing at the end of the hallway with a puzzled look on her face. Tobias' eyes locked with hers. Time seemed to stop as they both stood paralyzed, gazing intently into each other's eyes. Then, slowly, a troubled expression, yet still with a look of understanding, washed over Vanya's face.

Something nonverbal, and almost nonexistent, passed between the two of them as Vanya's expression of understanding transformed into one of utter sadness. Tobias held her gaze, feeling the warmth of her compassion, feeling the love for this woman who had been like a mother to him, in a way which felt so... *familiar.*

As the first teardrop slid down Vanya's cheek, Tobias broke their trance, taking the last step he needed to reach his destination. Then with a smooth and seemingly effortless motion, he slipped into Jesse's closet, pulled the door shut, and curled up on the floor.

ii

Amos Dewey and John Pinchot had felt honored when Luther had selected them to carry out such a simple, yet critical, task for the momentous occasion at hand. They were to apprehend, then prepare, a child living in the home of Jeffrey Chardin for the ordination of Luther as the Grand Elder.

As Dewey reached for the front doorknob of the Chardin home, Pinchot pulled him back.

"Hold it!" Pinchot whispered in a somewhat abrupt tone. "Before we go in, where is the kid's room?"

Dewey rolled his eyes. "How many times we gotta go over this, Pinchot? It's up the stairs, down the hall a little to the left, and then the first door on the right. And it's not a room, it's a closet!"

Pinchot nodded as his face flushed. Dewey had explained the procedure at least three times to him on the way over, but his nerves seemed to be getting the best of his short-term memory. Recollections of being caught burglarizing a house two years ago still loomed fresh in his mind.

It's not like we're breaking in or anything, he thought. *We have permission to enter!*

But then another, more ominous thought replaced it.

But they're going to kill this kid. Oh, man!

As if he could read his face, Dewey responded to Pinchot's fears.

"Listen," he reassured. "This kid was born for this purpose and this purpose only. He will be rewarded greatly by the Master for his sacrifice, as will we if we get off this damn doorstep!"

Pinchot winced at the last part of Dewey's statement. He nodded and reached for the doorknob.

It was unlocked, just as Luther had promised. They exchanged quick glances and then hastily located the staircase. Moving on ahead, Dewey slid up the steps with the grace of a deer. Pinchot's brief admiration was interrupted by a quick "psst", and a nasty "hurry up" stare from Dewey.

Pinchot followed, somewhat clumsily, up the steps. Dewey had already reached the designated door and motioned towards Pinchot's pouch.

Realization came over Pinchot as he reached into his pouch and pulled out a bottle of a chloroform-like substance (a concoction of the great Dr. Sanger). He carefully opened the top, then pulled a handkerchief out of his back pocket. Putting the handkerchief against the top of the bottle, he inverted the bottle three times. He then returned the top to the bottle and placed it back in his pouch.

Pinchot gave Dewey the "okay" sign. Dewey nodded and held up three fingers, two, one, then pulled the door swiftly, yet silently, open. Pinchot moved in, giving his eyes a moment to adjust, then quickly placed the handkerchief over the boy's mouth.

Surprisingly, the boy did not struggle. In fact, after removing the handkerchief, Pinchot felt the need to check for a pulse. Yes, it was there. The boy was out like a light.

Dewey pulled out a large bag, and the two of them stuffed the unconscious boy into it. Pulling the drawstring, Dewey picked up the bag over his shoulder. The two exchanged somewhat-relieved glances and then swiftly tiptoed down the stairs and out the front door.

They had done it—quickly and quietly. So quick, in fact, that they had failed to even notice the head of a small boy peering out into the hallway from the bedroom down the hall.

iii

While his subjects worked diligently to prepare the arrangements, Luther sat back in his room reading his predecessor's *Book of Shadows*. Visions of grandeur danced in his head as he slowly absorbed the deepest thoughts of the man who had founded the Brotherhood so many years before.

SEED

He turned the page, meditating over thoughts and reflections written more than six years ago. Upon reaching a particular section, Luther suddenly sat up with a start. His eyes widened in disbelief. Due to his gifting of second sight, he was not accustomed to being surprised. Yet what he read in the pages before him sent an unfamiliar chill through his body, with a foreign sense of foolishness to boot.

> **At the request of Father Luther, I contacted the Temple of Shaat to secure an appropriate tutor for his son. After considerable prayer and meditation, we have selected a former teacher, Vanessa Ami-Richards, for this task. Sister Vanessa will be...**

Ami-Richards. *Vanessa Ami-Richards.* Luther's hands began to shake as he dropped the *Book of Shadows.* Sweeping his left hand across his desk, he sent a crystal goblet careening, instantly smashing against the wall as he let out a thunderous wail.

Two of Luther's servants, Aleister Mazzini and Szandor Pike, rushed into the room. The taller of the two, Aleister, spoke, his voice shaking.

"Father? Is...is everything all right?"

Luther looked up, instinctively contemplating releasing his rage upon the two. However, he quickly pulled himself together, attempting to think rationally. After all, he was to be Grand Elder this night.

"Have Dewey and Pinchot returned with the boy?" he questioned, gritting his teeth.

"Ah...yes, Father. They had just pulled into the parking lot when we heard...ah... when we heard you call out."

"Are you familiar with the preparation procedures for the boy?"

The smaller of the two, Szandor, spoke this time. "Yes, Father. I am familiar with the procedures."

Luther was finally able to provide a trace of a grin, though it was admittedly contrived. "Very well. The two of you will be responsible for preparing the boy then. Send Dewey and Pinchot back to the house. Tell them to kill the woman."

"Father?" Aleister blurted out, then instantly wishing he had not.

Luther's eyes widened. "NOW, you fools! We have very little time!"

The two men, not wishing to see what would happen if they had to be told twice, shot out of the room and down the steps.

Luther clasped his arms behind his back and walked out from behind his desk, admiring the large tapestry of the beast punishing a priest in a sea of fire. He again grinned, this time with greater sincerity, as he shook his head.

"I salute you, Vanya. You really came close to pulling this off. You have been an admirable and worthy adversary."

iv

Vanya felt herself floating over a dreamy image. Slowly the picture came more into focus and subsequently her feet touched ground. She was standing in a large room where a dozen or so old men in brown robes knelt in prayer.

Dazzling light poured in from openings in the walls where she would have expected windows. As bright as the light was, however, it did not blind her. As she looked on, another robed figure entered the room, kneeling at the edge of the circle formed by the other men.

He pulled back his hood, and Vanya gasped. Though it had been nearly seven years since she had seen his face, there was no question in her mind who the man was who knelt before her. It was the meticulously dressed man from her vision of Jesse so long ago.

As Vanya stood, frozen in place, she realized she was now standing in the center of the circle formed by the robed men. The man from her vision looked up from his prayer, straight into Vanya's eyes. He spoke in a voice that revealed great strength and conviction.

"IT IS TIME!"

Vanya sat up with a jolt. She was in her bed. She turned to her clock, which read 11:37 p.m. What had happened?

She was disoriented. The last thing she could remember was... was... *Tobias!*

SEED

Vanya jumped out of bed and sprinted for Jesse's closet. Her heart sunk as she saw that his door was open, and he was nowhere to be found.

Vanya dashed, silently praying, towards Tobias' room. She reached it to find no one. She covered her mouth with her hand to prevent a scream. As she looked down the stairway, she saw the front door hanging wide open.

She stumbled down the steps and broke for the door to the garage, screaming, "No, God please, NO!"

21

"Lord, there is none like you!
You have broken the chains that bound me
I will sacrifice in your honour."

– St. Augustine
Confessions

i

Jesse had run a good quarter-mile from his house, desperately trying to catch up to the car that had sped from his home with his brother. He was out of breath and slowed to a walk when he saw the car turn a mile or so ahead of him.

Jesse was pretty sure they had gone to that place where his stepfather worked, called the "Temple". As he resumed a slow jog, he tried to remember how he had gotten into his brother's bed. Was Tobias playing a game with him? And he could not figure out why the men had thrown his brother in a bag. He was pretty certain these were bad men, and though he was frightened, Jesse was determined to get his brother back.

After perhaps another ten minutes of walking, he turned the corner and could now see the buildings in the town area. He could just make out the building at the beginning of the town called the Temple. If he ran, he could probably reach it in another ten minutes.

Jesse started to jog, but then spotted a set of headlights pulling out of the parking lot ahead and moving towards him. He hesitated for a moment, then jumped off into a ditch by the side of the road, hiding in the darkness.

The car sped past him, and Jesse recognized it as the same car that had taken his brother. The car swung a hard left, as if in a rush to retrace its own steps, and accelerated onward.

He hesitated. Were they bringing his brother back home? He couldn't be sure. After a moment of thought, he decided that if they were indeed returning Tobias home, then everything would be okay. But if they weren't, Tobias was somewhere in that building where the car pulled out of.

Jesse decided to check out the building and resumed his sprint towards it, seeking a reunion with his brother, friend, and protector.

ii

Szandor and Aleister laid the bag out on the table in the room just behind the altar. Szandor began opening the sack at one end.

"If I didn't know better," Aleister began, "I'd say Dewey was turned-on when I told him that he was supposed to off the lady!"

Szandor chuckled. "Yeah, but I'd swear on my mother's grave that Pinchot pissed his pants!"

Aleister let out a loud guffaw as Szandor pulled the sack off of the unconscious boy. Aleister's laugh quickly died out as his expression transformed into a look of puzzlement.

"Szandor?" he asked in a tentative voice.

Szandor was already reaching for the ceremonial wardrobe.

"Yeah, what?"

"Did you ever meet Chardin's kids?"

Szandor continued to pull items from the closet. "No. Why do you ask?"

"Well, I met the twins maybe three years ago, and I could have sworn Jesse was the one with *blond* hair."

Szandor turned and looked at the dark-haired boy lying on the table. He shrugged his shoulders.

"Kids' hair color can change pretty quickly. I wouldn't worry about it. You said it was a few years, right?"

"Yeah, but—"

"So maybe that's what happened. And maybe you were even mistaken about which kid was which."

DOMINION

"Shoot, Szandor, I don't think—"

"Listen, Aleister," Szandor snapped, obviously getting a bit perturbed over the conversation. "Both Dewey and Pinchot knew Jeffrey and the kids real well. They may not be Albert Einsteins, but they're not that stupid!"

Aleister looked down and then nodded. He must have been mistaken. The entire thing had probably shaken him up a bit, and his mind was reeling.

Aleister took the ceremonial head mask from Szandor and placed it over the head of the boy, lining up the eyeholes with the boy's eyes. He looked up at the clock, which read 11:51 p.m. They would have to hurry, as the ceremony was about to begin.

iii

Dewey and Pinchot kicked the front door in, their weapons drawn. Pinchot motioned to Dewey, and then sprinted up the steps. They looked towards Vanya's room and surprisingly did not detect any movement.

They crept cautiously towards the door, which was open only a crack. Pinchot glanced at Dewey, who carried a look of concerned suspicion on his face. He slowly pushed the door open. As he looked in, he could see the distinct figure of a woman lying in the bed.

Pinchot and Dewey simultaneously aimed their weapons and fired nearly a dozen rounds each into the figure. Pinchot flipped on the lights and moved cautiously towards the bed. In one quick motion, he swept the sheets off his prey.

"Dammit!" he cursed out loud as he looked upon what was left of the series of pillows that fell out of the bed.

Dewey looked to Pinchot. "Luther is going to have our asses!"

Pinchot did not respond. He was looking at a note taped to the lampshade. It read:

Dear Bad Guys,
    Some even badder guys were already here.
    See you in hell!

SEED

The last sound Dewey and Pinchot heard was the ringing of a telephone.

iv

Mikhail Ostankino put the cellular phone down in his car as he watched the house rapidly become engulfed in flames. Andrey Gavrilenkov sat next to him in the passenger side, with Vanya sobbing between Alexandre Nesterov and Yerik in the back.

"For God's sake, Father!" she cried. "We've got to find the boys!"

Nesterov nodded to Ostankino, who hit the accelerator with authority. The car sped off only moments before the roof of the Chardin house collapsed.

22

Things not what they used to be
Missing one inside of me
Deathly lost, this can't be real
Cannot stand this hell I feel

Emptiness is filling me
To the point of agony
Growing darkness taking dawn
I was me, but now he is gone.

– Metallica
Fade to Black

i

Luther stood in the center of the pentagram facing east, adorned in an immaculate red robe and wearing the headdress of a goat. He was surrounded by the remaining members of the Supreme Council, all clad in black hooded robes.

The Temple was filled beyond capacity, with nearly three hundred worshipers representing forty-seven Covens of the Brotherhood in attendance. Over a thousand lit candles served as the only light source in the hall.

Luther began to chant, followed by a response from the Supreme Council. The worshipers responded with a brief chant of their own, repeated three times in unison. So engrossed were the members of the congregation in the event that they did not even notice the small protrusion in the tapestry hanging above the upper balcony, which Jesse had slipped behind only moments earlier.

The Supreme Council opened their circle, leaving a clear path between Luther and the altar, approximately forty feet away on a raised platform. On one side of the altar stood an inverted cross with an image of a goat's head directly opposite it. In the center lay the book, *The Mother of Majesty*. With each step Luther took, the Supreme Council chanted a different syllable.

Upon reaching the platform, the congregation cheered in yet another sequence of syllables. Luther removed the goat's headdress and nodded to a man with a drum to his left. As the drum began to beat, the congregation separated into two even parts. A procession of a dozen men robed and hooded in dark purple entered, holding a platform high above their heads. On the platform lay a young boy, a ceremonial head mask on his head and wearing pure white robes.

Jesse looked on in amazement as he instantly realized this was his brother, Tobias. But why wasn't he moving? Surely he couldn't sleep with all this racket. Too confused and frightened to move, Jesse looked on.

As the procession reached the altar, the boy was placed across it in front of Luther. His hands and feet were then bound, each to a different corner. The boy seemed to show some signs of consciousness at this point, starting a slow roll with his head.

Luther looked down at one of the figures clad in purple and nodded. The figure removed his hood, revealing the face of Jeffrey Chardin. Jeffrey moved forward towards Luther, hesitantly at first, and then from his robe he removed a nine-inch blade studded with a number of precious jewels. He handed the knife to Luther before slowly backing away until he was back within the pentagram.

Jesse let out a sigh of relief when one of the robed people removed his hood, revealing his stepfather. He knew that his stepfather had always been extremely protective of Tobias and would not let anyone harm a hair on his head. Jesse strained his eyes, trying to see what his stepfather had handed Luther.

Something else began to transpire as Luther continued to recite incantations. Jesse watched as twenty or so "blurs" appeared in a semicircle behind Luther. They began to come more and more into focus, and Jesse could see that these were figures of men. Yet he could still see through them. Luther's image even seemed to blur at that moment. Jesse suppressed a tremendous urge to cry out.

Luther looked down across the boy lying on the altar, watching his eyelids begin to flicker. He held out the knife with both hands as the horde chanted on in perfect unison. The Supreme Council moved up to the altar, completing the circle started by the now fully materialized *Illumini*.

The chanting continued and grew louder, as did the beating of the drums. Luther closed his eyes, grasping the handle of the blade with both hands. He slowly raised the knife above his head, whispering unheard incantations to himself. A grin spread across his face as his eyes opened. Mesmerized by the chanting, so focused upon the moment, he did not even here the delicate voice of a child screaming.

"Nooooooooooooooooooo!" Jesse let out with all his might; finally realizing what was about to happen to his brother.

Nearly half the congregation did hear him and looked up towards the balcony, where they saw a half-naked, terrified boy looking down. There was no immediate recognition of the boy, with the exception of one member.

Jeffrey looked up towards the barely audible sound he had heard from the balcony. A startled and confused look came over his face as he spotted Jesse's terrified gaze looking down at him. Jeffrey paused, only for a second, and was then hit by a realization so strong he would have sworn his stomach exploded.

Jeffrey swung his head back towards the altar and screamed with a voice that could be heard even above the rising din.

"TOBIAS!"

Tobias felt himself slowly awaken from a dream. This was different though, his head felt like it weighed a thousand pounds. He tried to move his arms and legs but quickly realized he could not.

He blinked hard. Everything was still blurry. He was hearing noises like a soundtrack that was running ten speeds too slow. Slowly, Tobias was able to start focusing on the figure above him. He could see the color red, but he soon realized that there was something between him and this figure. Like he was looking out through some sort of peephole.

He could now distinguish the sound of drums, and many people talking, yet altogether, like when they said prayers in church. Maybe that was where he was—church! He had fallen asleep again in church!

However, this thought was quickly dismissed as his eyes came into nearly full focus. He now realized the man he was looking at was Luther, and he could feel the sensation that he was lying on his back. Tobias looked up to see Luther smile and then open his own eyes.

From out of the now unbearable chanting, he could have sworn he heard his father call his name. He watched Luther grimace and bring his hands down.

Tobias experienced a sharp, tremendous pain in his chest. He felt his lungs and throat fill with fluid as his vision began to blur. This was a horrible dream from which he prayed he would soon awaken. But instead of returning to reality, his consciousness began to fade until there was nothing left but darkness.

Jesse stood frozen, not being able to accept what he had just witnessed. He saw his father sprint towards the altar. Luther, not aware of the commotion, looked up and met eyes with Jesse. For a split-second, a look of confusion came over his face. But in the next instant, he pointed towards Jesse and bellowed, "Get him!"

Jesse, still unable to move, suddenly felt a figure engulf him and pull him from his feet. He felt himself being jerked around, banging through other people. The stench of the figure carrying him snapped him out of his temporary shock like a smelling salt. Jesse began to fight against the figure.

As they dashed out into the second floor hallway, Jesse realized that they were not running *to* the other members, but instead *away* from them. They darted down the right corridor, yet stopped on a dime as Jesse looked up to see hooded figures coming their way.

They made a quick reverse turn, moving forward several steps before they again stopped, additional members of the horde closing in on them. Jesse screamed.

With a final half-turn, Jesse found himself looking at a large picture stained-glass window. After a moment's hesitation, with Jesse in hand, the figure accelerated towards the window.

There was a crash, and Jesse felt himself falling. The figure clenched him tighter, and in an instant Jesse felt his body push hard into that of this other figure. They were no longer moving. He heard several snaps.

Shards of broken glass fell upon them, and Jesse felt a sharp pain in his side. He struggled to get up as he heard the sound of a car screeching to a halt. He looked up to see headlights no more than five feet away from him.

As he heard the car doors opening, Jesse reached down to pull a nine-inch shard from his side, cutting both hands as he did so. He quickly got up, ready to resume his aided flight, but then he recognized his Nanny Vanya emerging from the car with an expression of terror on her face.

Jesse ran to her, cutting his feet on the broken glass. He leapt into her arms and felt her strength pull him against her. But just as quickly as he felt the comfort of her hug, he sensed her body become rigid.

Jesse looked up to see Vanya's gaze fixed on the figure that lay on the ground amidst the broken glass. Though his body was severely injured and his face was now covered with blood, Vanya instantly recognized the shabbily dressed man from her visions.

He looked up at her with the eyes of someone who had seen several thousand years.

"Vanya," he whispered. "You must go now."

His voice was straining, yet still held a commanding tone.

"But I've got to find Tob—"

"Tobias is gone," the man interjected in between coughs. "You must leave this place *now*!"

Though Vanya was not ready to accept this, she heard her father's voice and was rudely yanked into the car with Jesse still clutching to her side. The car spun its tires as they accelerated away from the now riotous crowd emerging from the building.

Vanya sat in shock, no longer aware of reality. Lying in her lap, desperately seeking comfort, was Jesse, repeating the same name over and over and over.

"Toby..."

SEED

ii

Father Daniel quivered as an intense pressure exerted itself upon his lungs to the point he was nearly unable to breathe. He intensified his focus on the crucified Christ, and suddenly vomited violently.

Sweat poured from his glands like someone who had just had a high fever break.

Father Daniel gasped as his breath returned. Whatever force he had sacrificed against, now in his tenth day, was broken.

iii

He pulled the emergency vehicle up to the backside of the pagan Temple. He had not used the flashing lights or siren so as to arrive unnoticed. Yet it was clear that that would not be a problem, as a great commotion was taking place at the front of the Temple. He stole a brief glance in that direction as a car suddenly screeched away from a pursuing mob.

I am too late?

He threw the vehicle into park and jumped out, moving briskly towards the back door. He had been delayed. While hastening to arrive to this event, a woman carrying a child within her womb had stepped out in front of the emergency vehicle. He had been unable to stop quickly enough and had glanced the expecting woman, sending her sprawling unconscious to the pavement. Despite the urgency of his mission, he could not leave her there.

As he tended to the woman, watching her vital signs continue to plummet, she suddenly opened her eyes, looked up to him with a furtive smile, and then vanished. He returned to his vehicle mystified, only to find it would not start. Ten minutes later, the engine finally turned over.

The limitations here are too great!

He approached the door to the Temple, and realizing that every moment counted, did not wait to check if it was locked. He passed through it.

The worship area was empty, though he could still hear the shouts from outside. There on the altar lay the boy.

He stepped up onto the dais, his heart racing. The gaping wound in the boy's chest was evident; there was no sign of movement.

I am too late.

A wave of deep sadness enveloped him, yet he did not allow it to dissuade him from his task. He lifted the head mask off of the motionless boy and then involuntarily dropped it in utter astonishment.

This was not as he had expected. Still, he would not permit another instant to pass. He reached out his right hand, placing it on the boy's chest, and closing his eyes, permitted a light, mystic melody to emerge from his lips.

There was a sudden, and unexpected, warm breeze that swept past him, as his ears—his spirit—detected another melody... from behind him? This was not a harmonizing accompaniment, however. It was a... a... *counter* melody.

He tried to turn but was unable to do so. He felt the sensation of being bound by numerous fetters, first in his feet, then his legs, moving up through his torso, until even the song from his lips had to cease.

The boy's body jerked as the man sensed an overpowering presence behind him. He struggled to free himself as he felt its breath upon the nape of his neck.

23

"In the long run, we are all dead."

– John Maynard Keynes

i

The morning had been sultry, and the crowd began to dissipate from the gravesite once the service had been completed. One man remained, tearfully moving to the edge of the smaller than usual dig.

Jeffrey looked down at the small casket and broke down, falling to his knees. A light drizzle began to fall.

"Oh Tobias... Oh my Tobias..."

Delving into the self-obsessed depths of his own grief, Jeffrey barely noticed the figure that now stood at the opposite side of the grave. The figure spoke in a somewhat caring tone.

"It is a real shame, yes, Jeffrey?" he said.

Jeffrey looked up, slowly, still crying. The man spoke with a thick accent... it sounded...

"I...I've lost everything," he replied.

The man shook his head as another approached from behind him holding an umbrella over this man's head.

"Jeffrey, Jeffrey, Jeffrey," the man began in a condescending tone. "I do not think you fully understand the meaning of loss as of yet. That is why I am here—to help you understand."

Jeffrey looked at the man inquisitively. "H-How do you know my name?"

The man chuckled sadly, again shaking his head. "What kind of man would not know the name of his own son-in-law?"

The puzzled look on Jeffrey's face turned to one of horrific realization. He was done for, and he knew it. He couldn't fight anymore. He dropped his head with an expression of surrender on his face.

"M-Mr. Nesterov," he mumbled, no longer maintaining eye contact.

Alexandre Nesterov smiled solemnly. Jeffrey was now aware of two more men in suits standing behind him. One sucked heavily on a cigarette as the other chomped away loudly on his gum.

"Very good, Jeffrey, you show... promise!"

Jeffrey again looked up, the tears now streaming from his face. He looked confused.

"P-Promise?"

"Yes, Jeffrey," Nesterov responded. "The promise of redemption. You see, Jeffrey, in my country there was the Party, and then there was the family. Well, I guess you could say 'the party is over', so we are left to only care for the family. Now you, Jeffrey, you have caused my family a great deal of pain over the past few years. I am now standing over the grave of a grandson I never met..." Nesterov's jaw clenched; he was slowly losing the ability to maintain his composure. "...and next to him rests a daughter I loved. And now I have to watch two people I care about very dearly spend the rest of their lives in fear. *Fear*, Jeffrey, do you understand what I have gone through in my life so that my family would *not* have to ever fear again? I do not believe you do. Are you following me, Jeffrey?"

"Y-Yes sir," Jeffrey responded. He heard the sound of a large engine starting and now saw another man in a suit driving a backhoe towards the pile of soil left from the digging of Tobias's grave. He again looked down, wiping his eyes.

"You see, Jeffrey," Nesterov continued, but stopped momentarily as his eye was caught by a small tree that seemed out of place only twenty feet or so from the grave. Yet before he would allow another thought to pass, he looked back to Jeffrey. "I do not like pain, and by pain I mean the kind that is inside of you, slowly tearing away at your very soul. Have you ever read the Bible, Jeffrey? Of course not, what was I thinking? Well, anyway, there is this passage that says something to the point of, 'If it is your eye that is your problem, pluck it out, for it is better to enter the Kingdom of God with one eye than to see with both in the eternal fire'. As you can see, Jeffrey, I need to pluck out the source of my pain. Can you guess who that is, Jeffrey?"

Jeffrey, still looking down, nodded solemnly.

"Jeffrey, do not get me wrong though. This has nothing to do with business. This is a family matter. And personally, Jeffrey, I do not think you have been spending enough quality time with your son." Nesterov's jaw clenched, and he said the final words through his teeth. "Would you not like to spend some more quality time with Tobias?"

Jeffrey started to cry as he sensed the two men behind him move closer. And with his last grain of hope, he spoke the final words of his tormented life, mere echoes at this point, of his difficult, yet still happier childhood days:

"F-Forgive me... *Father*... forgive me... for... for I have... sinned..."

ii

It had been near two weeks since Father Daniel had been released from the intense prayer he had engaged in for a period of ten days. He continued to carry a deep sense of sadness, but these melancholic feelings were mitigated by a sense that these sufferings, though tragic, were being permitted by the Almighty as part of a greater plan. He had done what was asked of him.

Walking amidst the early morning business rush, Father Daniel turned onto the next street and into the South Philadelphia neighborhood that had become primarily ethnic Japanese-American. Just a month earlier, St. Maximilian Kolbe Blessed Sacrament Chapel had been dedicated and consecrated, and he was honored to have been placed in charge of this jewel in the midst of a part of the city which had fallen into disrepair.

When he was within thirty yards of the entrance, Father Daniel stopped suddenly. His mind nearly swooned as he saw, amidst the throng of comers and goers, a young boy of no more than seven years standing at the base of the chapel steps, gazing intently at him. The boy stood out dramatically in this part of town, looking of Mediterranean descent, yet even more oddly, he was dressed in a small black cassock, not unlike an altar boy. The people continued to move busily about the sidewalk and streets, not seeming to notice the unusual scene before them.

The boy looked, with eyes unmistakably sad, across the street. There, was another image that seemed out of place. An olive-skinned street vendor was rolling his vending machine awkwardly along the sidewalk. He did not seem interested in selling anything to anyone, however, keeping his head low, though his eyes darted back and forth nervously. The casing he pushed seemed to be of much greater weight than what would be expected, and it was obvious that the vendor was exerting a great deal of energy pushing it.

Father Daniel's eyes turned back to the boy.

"Will you not come visit Me?"

Did the boy speak? He was not sure, but it was then that the familiar maternal presence engulfed him. The boy turned and walked into the chapel through the supposedly locked door. Father Daniel again glanced towards the vendor across the street, who had now situated his vending machine directly across from the chapel and then got down on his knees. Still distracted by the surreal nature of the scene, Father Daniel hurried to the chapel door. He reached for the doorknob...

Locked! What in...?

He fumbled for his keys, feeling a sense of urgency, then inserted them into the lock and burst into the tiny chapel. A quick scan of the scene found the structure empty. Upon further attention, Father Daniel was surprised to find the monstrance containing the Blessed Sacrament exposed on the altar. Then he again heard the familiar maternal voice within his heart.

"Daniel... prostrate yourself before my Son..."

Without hesitation, Daniel closed the door behind him and did as he was told. The moment his face touched the ground...

...the Earth shook.

Father Daniel clenched his eyes shut as the sound of a thousand chariots rumbled through the land and a great rush of hot wind passed over him. Millions of shards of broken stained glass fell upon him as a sense of zero gravity enveloped his body. Then, as suddenly as it began, the world was blanketed with an eerie silence.

Father Daniel stood. The structure of the chapel was still intact, and the monstrance and altar unmoved. Yet the door and stain-glassed windows were completely gone. Father Daniel's eyes widened as he gasped, "Father in Heaven..."

For a radius of at least three hundred yards, save the chapel, not a single structure remained standing.

SEED

Father Daniel fell to his knees and began to weep. He no longer felt the maternal presence and a single thought continued to invade his consciousness.

What hath man wrought?

Citations

Chap	Reference
	New Testament Scripture, Matthew 13: 24-30, directly translated from the Greek.
1	Eliot, Thomas Stearns. *The Hollow Men, Poems: 1909-1925*, T.S. Eliot, 1925.
2	Gibran, Khalil. (*b*. January 6, 1883, *d*. April 10, 1931).
3	Aeschylus. *Prometheus Bound, ca* 430 BC.
6	Agee, James. *Let Us Now Praise Famous Men,* John T. Mill/Houghton Mifflin, 1988.
7	Milton, John. (*b*. December 9, 1608, *d*. November 8, 1674).
8	Titus Lucretius Carus. (*b*. ca 99 B.C., *d*. ca 55 B.C.).
9	Dickinson, Emily. (*b*. December 10, 1830, *d*. May 15, 1886).
10	Lewis, Clive Staples. *The Screwtape Letters*, *C.S. Lewis* New York: Pte Ltd/HarperCollins, 1996.
13	Jones, John Paul, Page, Jimmy, & Plant, Robert (Led Zeppelin). "No Quarter", *Houses of the Holy*, Atlantic, 1973.
15	Shakespeare, William. *Macbeth*, (*b*. ca 1564, *d*. April 23, 1616).
18	Morrison, James Douglas (The Doors), "Not to Touch the Earth", *Waiting for the Sun*, Rhino/wea, 1968.
21	Augustine of Hippo (Saint), *Confessions*, (*b*. November 13, 354, *d*. August 28, 430).
22	Hetfield, James, Ulrich, Lars, Burton, Cliff, Hammett, Kirk (Metallica). "Fade to Black", *Ride the Lightning*, Megaforce Records,1984.
23	Keynes, John Maynard. "A Tract on Monetary Reform", 1923.

For additional information on authors, artists, works, and quotes cited in *Dominion* (including the ability to purchase) please visit www.thedominionproject.com/citations.html.

The Dominion Project continues with Book II

PHOENIX

Vanishing Dawn

Jonathan and Nathan have been best friends since their first contentious meeting in the seventh grade, yet all would agree that these graduating seniors are an unlikely pair. Jonathan excels in both academics and athletics, while Nathan approaches life as an irreverent free spirit, not finding anything or anyone worth taking too seriously. Yet despite their affable natures, each carries his own dark secret; personal demons from their unique pasts which they do not dare share even with each other. Their hidden lives are exposed as Luther re-enters the maelstrom, seeking to recover that which he has made a claim – the very soul of his son, Jesse.

Order your copy at

www.thedominionproject.com

Also available; *Dominion Interlude: Reader's Companions* with character sketches, book summaries, references and more!

Direct Ordering of the Dominion Series

Especially for those who do not have online access, all books can be purchased direct from T.C.C./Sacrata Dei Press by mail.

Dominion – The Series

Book I: Seed	*(June 2009)*
Book II: Phoenix	*(July 2009)*
Book III: Tryst	*(August 2009)*
Book VI: Requiem	*(October 2009)*
Book V: Ascension	*(December 2009)*
Book VI: Abyss	*(May 2010)*
Book VII: Revelation	*(January 2011)*

Dominion – Reference

For the Dominion reading enthusiast who wishes to delve deeper into the series, these brief reader's companions/reference are a helpful tool providing character profiles, time and location references, summaries, background, and descriptions. Each Interlude is meant to follow its corresponding book from the series, offering a more in-depth understanding of the "Dominion world" while further preparing the reader for the next book.

First Interlude
Second Interlude
Third Interlude
Fourth Interlude
Fifth Interlude
Sixth Interlude
Coda: Deux Ex Machina

Please call (574) 307-0413 for current mailing address, shipping rates, and tax rates (where applicable). Once obtained, please identify in your mailing your name and address, which book(s) you are ordering and the quantity, and provide a check or money order in U.S. dollars made payable to T.C.C./Sacrata Dei Press.